D0091030

For Whom the Funeral Bell Tolls

Livia J. Washburn

FOR WHOM THE FUNERAL BELL TOLLS Copyright © February 2012 by Livia J. Washburn.

ISBN-13: 978-1470050306
ISBN-10: 1470050307

The Delilah Dickinson Literary Tour
Mystery Series

Frankly My Dear I'm Dead

Huckleberry Finished

Killer On a Hot Tin Roof

For Whom The Funeral Bell Tolls

For James, Shayna
and Joanna

Chapter 1

Ernest Hemingway once defined courage as "grace under pressure".

However, Papa never had to ride herd on a bunch of drunken, horny tourists.

No, that job fell to me, and I'd had just about enough of it, especially with the way rock music was pounding from the speakers in Sloppy Joe's Bar so that everybody crowded in there shoulder to shoulder had to yell to be heard.

Somebody bumped into me from behind, and since the bar was right in front of me, there was nowhere for me to go. The crowd pressed him against me so intimately that all concept of personal space was demolished, and it got even worse when a familiar voice gulped in my ear, "Oh, cripes! I'm sorry, Miz D!"

I turned my head to look over my shoulder at Luke Edwards. Even in the garish light of the famous watering hole, I could see that his face was flaming red with embarrassment.

"That's all right, Luke," I told him. "If you can't dry-hump your mother-in-law in Key West, who can you . . . Oh, never mind!"

That just made him even more flustered. I knew it would, and saying it might have been a little mean. But I was feeling more than a little flustered myself. It seemed like we were almost at the end of the world, and the normal rules didn't apply here. My rambunctious clients seemed to feel the same way.

There were an even dozen of them. We had rendezvoused that afternoon at a Miami hotel, then made the long drive down through the Keys on Highway One in a fifteen-passenger van with Luke at the wheel.

Counting Luke and me, there were fourteen people on this tour. We could have brought along one more, but that would have meant having thirteen clients, and even though I don't consider myself a superstitious person, I wasn't just about to do that. No way.

Considering the way some of the tours I'd put together in the past had gone, I didn't think it was a good idea to tempt fate.

By the time we'd driven more than a hundred miles from Miami and checked into our hotel, the Bradenton Beach Resort, it was too late to do any sightseeing, but not too late for the clients to enjoy some of Key West's notorious nightlife. They were eager to do exactly that, so after they'd freshened up, they piled back into the van and we headed for Key West's Old Town, the most historic – and most lively – part of this island that had once been known as Bone Key, because of the skeletons that early Spanish explorers found on it.

I couldn't help but hope that wasn't an omen.

Not that I wanted to dwell on the possibility of trouble, but when you put together tours devoted to famous literary figures and folks keep getting murdered on them . . . well, there's an old saying about how you're not paranoid if they're really out to get you.

Not all of my tours featured a corpse, of course. That would just be silly, and a good sign that I ought to get out of the business. But it had happened often enough that Delilah Dickinson Literary Tours (that's me, my daughter Melissa, and her husband Luke) had a reputation that scared off some people. I tried to make up for that by putting together really good and affordable tours, like this Ernest Hemingway-themed visit to Key West.

Next to the Hemingway House itself, Sloppy Joe's was probably the most famous place in Key West because Hemingway had spent a lot of time drinking with the place's colorful owner Joe Russell. As I had explained to the clients on the way there, local legend had it that Hemingway had once received a $1000 royalty check for *A Farewell to Arms* from his publisher in New York while he was living in Key West, and the bank had refused to cash it because nobody who worked there believed that the scruffy beachcomber who brought in the check was really a famous author. But Joe Russell, the proprietor of Sloppy Joe's, had cashed it and earned himself Hemingway's enduring friendship.

It was a nice story, and it had the ring of truth to it. Of course, we weren't in the original Sloppy Joe's, where Papa had sat around and drank with Joe Russell. That location was a few blocks away and now housed another watering hole called Captain Tony's Saloon. But this version of Sloppy Joe's catered to the tourists by billing itself as Hemingway's Favorite Bar, and the marketing worked. People who came to Key West for the whole Hemingway experience flocked here. It was loud and rowdy and sexy, too, which didn't hurt.

The pressure of the crowd finally eased enough for Luke to extricate himself from close proximity to my backside. He slid into a narrow open space beside me at the bar and said, "Lord have mercy, Miz D, I never meant to get so, uh, familiar."

"Don't worry about it, Luke," I told him. "It's so crowded in here a girl could wind up gettin' pregnant and never even realize she'd been havin' fun."

"Yeah, I guess so." He stood a little taller and craned his neck to look around the room at the nightly chaos. "I can't see all of our clients anymore."

"Doesn't matter. They're all grown. Some of 'em will probably want to wander around Old Town some." I patted the pocket of my slacks. "I've got all their numbers in my phone, and if they're not back at the van by eleven-thirty, I'll call 'em and tell them to get there unless they want to walk all the way back to the beach."

It wasn't that much of a walk, fifteen minutes or so, but on a hot, muggy night it would take a lot out of you, and all the nights were hot and muggy in Key West. Life here at the southernmost tip of the United States was lubricated equally by booze and sweat.

I was drinking bottled water, and I signaled the bartender to bring me another one. He was a muscular, gorgeous young man with long dark hair and a tight black T-shirt. He actually had a gold ring in one ear, giving him a piratical look. I recalled that at one time, a man wearing a ring in his ear like that supposedly meant he was gay, but I didn't know if that still applied or if it was even true. Not that it mattered in this case, because all I wanted from this young man was another bottle of water.

He grinned at me as he slid it across the bar and made the five dollar bill I put down disappear. "In town on a tour?" he asked, raising his voice to be heard over the blaring music.

"That's right." I didn't bother explaining that I was in charge of the tour, not one of the paying customers.

His grin took in Luke as he said, "I hope you and your friend enjoy it."

"Business associate," I said as I pointed a thumb at Luke.

"Uh-huh," the bartender said. "Well, if you and your business associate need somebody to show you around after-hours, I wouldn't mind."

His eyes did a slow crawl over me, then gave Luke the same treatment.

I swallowed hard. "Thanks, but I don't think that'll be necessary."

"Suit yourself," he said, still grinning. He moved off down the bar to take care of some other customers.

Luke leaned closer to me and said, "Miz D, was he *hitting* on you?"

"Well, you don't have to say it like it's the most far-fetched thing in the world. Anyway, I think he was hittin' on both of us."

Luke frowned. "What are you . . . You mean . . . Whoa!" He looked around. "What kind of a town is this?"

"Free-spirited," I told him.

"I'll say. And he thought that you and I – "

"Again, don't push it."

"Okay, okay. Guess I'd better circulate and make sure none of our folks need anything."

"Be discreet," I told him. "Some people come on tours like this because they're romantic."

"I don't see how anybody could be romantic in a madhouse like this."

I thought he had a point, actually. I would have found it a lot more romantic strolling along one of the white sandy beaches scattered around the key, hand in hand with somebody I cared about. Problem was, I didn't have anybody like that right now. Back home in Atlanta, I'd been dating Dr. Will Burke off and on for a couple of years – he's the literature professor sort of doctor, not the medical kind – but we were more off than on at the moment.

I figured that was mostly my fault. At my age, with one divorce behind me, even a largely amicable one, I was a little commitment-shy. I had a reasonably successful business and an adorable daughter and son-in-law who were going to make me a grandma one of these days. I didn't really need any more in my life than that, did I?

Luke wandered off into the crowd. I sipped on my bottled water and did some people-watching. And there were all kinds of people to watch, let me tell you. Key West drew them from all over, all ages and shapes and sizes. I saw gung-ho business types, male and female both, with Bluetooths in their ears and smart phones in their hands, prob-ably checking the overseas markets and making deals right here in the middle of Sloppy Joe's. Next to them were tie-dyed, sandals-and-granny-glasses-wearing sorts who looked like they were stuck in a time loop where it was perpetually 1967. Fishermen, artists, high rollers, tourists looking to lose the pallor of a Midwestern winter . . . every-body came to Key West sooner or later, and once they got here, everybody came to Sloppy Joe's.

I liked it. It was a good break for me, I thought, getting out of my comfort zone like this.

"Ms. Dickinson?"

The man's voice made me turn around. I was pretty good at putting names with faces, so even though I'd known them for only a few hours, I recognized George and Kerry Matheson. He was in plumbing supplies, the sort of balding former athlete who was starting to put on more than a few extra pounds, and she was a pretty, perky house-wife with short brown hair who looked like she could have played that part on a sitcom. Nice enough people, from what I knew of them so far.

"Ms. Dickinson, this is great!" George went on. "I love this place!"

"I'm glad you're enjoying yourself," I told him. "We'll have plenty of free time while we're here, so you can come back if you like or explore some of the other nightlife."

"Oh, I'm sure we will," he said. "Right, hon?"

Kerry nodded. She didn't look quite as en-thralled by Sloppy Joe's as her husband obviously was, but she seemed to be having a reasonably good time.

"I'm looking forward to seeing Hemingway's house tomorrow," she said.

We were going to be in Key West for four nights and three days. A visit to the Hemingway House was first on the itinerary the next morning, and the rest of the first two days would be devoted to seeing all the other historic sights and museums on the island. The third day would be free time for the clients to shop or just enjoy the beach and the other amenities of the resort where we were stay-ing. Then the next morning it would be back to

Miami, where we would all go our separate ways.

"It's really interesting, all right," I said in response to Kerry Matheson's comment. "I guess you must be a Hemingway fan."

She rolled her eyes. "Sure, but not as much as Mr. Harvick."

I knew what she meant. There were four couples on this tour and four singles, and Walter Harvick was one of the singles. He was as big a Hemingway fan as anybody I'd ever run into. In fact, he had told me that he'd been here to Key West half a dozen times before on his own, as well as visiting Hemingway's haunts in Paris, Spain, Cuba, and Idaho.

"But I thought it might be fun to see those places with a group for a change, so I'm starting here," he'd said to me in the van that afternoon.

I hoped he would enjoy himself. He probably wouldn't learn anything new, but that wouldn't matter to him. I knew from experience that certain readers who are really devoted to a particular author can go back again and again to the places where that writer produced his or her work. There was something about just being there that was special to them.

Then something happened that made me wonder if there really are such things as omens. Kerry Matheson had just mentioned Walter Harvick when Luke appeared beside me, touched my arm, and leaned close to me to say, "Trouble, Miz D! It's that Harvick fella, and I think he's about to get his butt whipped!"

Chapter 2

I turned to look at Luke, and the worry in his eyes told me he wasn't overreacting. One of my clients was in trouble, and it was my job to put a stop to it if I could.

"Where is he?" I asked.

"Over in the corner by those palm trees," Luke said.

Sloppy Joe's was the sort of place that had big potted palms for atmosphere. When I looked around I spotted a cluster of them in the corner Luke indicated.

"Let's go," I said.

Behind me, George Matheson asked, "Do you need some help, Ms. Dickinson?"

"George, this is none of our business," his wife said.

"Thanks, Mr. Matheson, but we've got this. Don't we, Luke?"

"Sure," Luke said. He had played ball in high school and college, too, and a lot more recently than Matheson had.

I nodded to him to indicate that he should go

first, then settled in close behind him as he cleared a path through the crowd. Even with Luke shouldering his way along, it took us a couple of minutes to make our way across the big main room of Sloppy Joe's.

I hoped we weren't going to be too late to help Mr. Harvick.

When we got there, Harvick was still on his feet, and I was grateful for that. The trouble wasn't over, though. A burly, middle-aged man with white hair and a beard stood in front of Harvick, poking him in the chest and yelling at him.

" – what the hell you're talking about!" the man said. "I'm a dead ringer for Papa, and everybody here knows it!"

"Not everybody," Harvick said. "I don't know it, because you don't really look like him. It takes more than white hair and a beard, you know. Anyway, when Hemingway lived here in the Thirties and Forties, he didn't look anything like you do. He still had dark hair and a mustache then."

"I won the Hemingway Lookalike Contest two years ago!"

"All that proves is that the judges were either blind or your cronies or both."

Walter Harvick had a mouth on him for a fella who probably weighed a hundred and forty pounds soaking wet. He looked like a mild and unassuming sort – about forty years old, curly brown hair that had started to thin, and a pretty weak chin, to be honest – but evidently he had the soul of a tiger when it came to his literary idol.

"Why, you weaselly little pipsqueak!" the Papa lookalike exploded.

I hadn't heard anybody called a pipsqueak in years. I didn't have time to think about that, however, because the man bunched up a fist and swung it at Harvick's head.

It's not that unusual for a tourist to get in a fight with a local. It can happen anywhere, on any tour. Luke had had experience with trouble like this. He got ready to jump the Hemingway lookalike and hang on to him so that he couldn't hurt Mr. Harvick. The bouncers who worked here at Sloppy Joe's would probably show up in a matter of seconds to take him off Luke's hands and escort him out.

As it turned out, though, Luke didn't have to do anything. Harvick ducked under the punch, then reached out and grabbed hold of the man's arm. He must have known a lot about pressure points and things like that, because it appeared that he didn't do anything except squeeze lightly on the man's arm. That was enough to make the man howl in pain and drop helplessly to his knees.

The bouncers were there even quicker than I expected them to be. Like the bartender who had flirted with Luke and me, they were big and wore tight black T-shirts.

One of them got in Harvick's face and said, "Let him go, buddy, right now."

"You don't understand," Harvick said. "He attacked me."

"Yeah, well, he's the one hurtin', so let go of him."

With a shrug, Harvick did what the bouncer told him. When he released the Hemingway look-alike's arm, the man went all the way to the floor, where he curled up and whimpered.

"Hemingway would have been disgusted by you," Harvick told him.

"Time for you to go," the other bouncer said as

he reached for Harvick.

I was afraid Harvick might try the same ninja trick on the bouncer, in which case he might get really hurt or at least arrested, and I didn't want either of those things happening.

So I stepped forward quickly and said over the pounding beat of the music, "Just a minute here, fellas. There's no need for any more trouble."

The bouncer who was reaching for Harvick stopped. He turned and glared at me as he asked, "Who the hell are you, lady?"

"My name's Delilah Dickinson," I told him. "I run a tour company, and Mr. Harvick here is one of my clients."

"So you're a glorified tour guide. That doesn't change anything here." The guy nodded toward the Hemingway lookalike, who was still curled up on the floor. "Rollie here is one of our regulars, and he's hurt."

"He took the first swing," Luke put in. "Mr. Harvick was just defending himself."

"Nobody asked you, frat boy."

Luke started to lose his temper, then he stopped and said, "You think I look young enough to be a frat boy? Really?"

I pushed forward again. "My associate is right," I insisted. "This wasn't my client's fault. The other man attacked him."

The second bouncer looked at Harvick and asked, "What'd you do to get Rollie so mad at you, anyway? He's usually pretty easy-going."

Harvick's narrow shoulders rose and fell in a shrug. "I just told him he didn't really look like Ernest Hemingway."

The bouncers exchanged a glance. One of them said, "Yeah, that'd do it."

"Look, we're gonna give you the benefit of the doubt, all right?" the other bouncer said to Harvick. "But only because we know that Rollie's pretty touchy about looking like Papa. But that's it. Any more trouble and you're outta here."

"I didn't start this trouble," Harvick protested.

"Yeah, you sorta did, by saying what you said."

That wasn't completely fair, since Harvick hadn't known how the local was going to react – and to be honest, the guy really didn't look all that much like Hemingway – but the bouncers had a point, too.

I moved in and linked arms with Harvick. "Why don't you come with me, Walter?" I suggested. "We'll go to the bar and get a drink."

He didn't pull away from me. He said, "Well, I suppose that would be all right . . ."

It sounds bad to say it, but Harvick wasn't exactly the type to have women paying a lot of attention to him. And while I'm no femme fatale, I think I clean up pretty nice. Halfway decent, anyway. So Harvick seemed to enjoy it as I hung on to him and stayed close while we made our way back across the crowded room, trailed by Luke. A glance over my shoulder told me that the bouncers were helping the lookalike to his feet.

"What in the world did you do to that man?" I asked, forcing a slightly gushing tone into my voice. "I never saw anything like it."

"Oh, it wasn't anything, really," Harvick said with a note of modesty that was just as false as the enthusiasm I'd just displayed. "I just exerted some force on one of his nerves. Anyone could have done it."

"Well, I couldn't have," I said.

Luke leaned forward and added, "I would've

punched him in the face."

"You must be some sort of cop to know how to do that," I said to Harvick.

"Oh, no, not at all. I'm an insurance adjuster."

"Well, I'm impressed anyway. That guy was big."

"But not tough. There's a difference between bluster and genuine toughness."

He was right about that, of course. Still, he had an air of smug self-satisfaction about him that rubbed me the wrong way. He acted like he didn't know how close he had come to going to jail, or at least getting tossed out into Duval Street.

"If you'd like, I could show you how to do that little trick . . ." he offered.

"No thanks," I said quickly. I'll flirt with a client if it's necessary to smooth over some trouble, but I draw the line at letting one of them paw me in the guise of showing me self-defense methods, which I was confident Harvick had in mind. "Let's get a drink instead."

"All right." We arrived at the bar, and Harvick told the bartender he wanted a rum punch. I still had most of my bottle of water, so I held it up to show the bartender I was fine. He was the same one who'd suggested that he was able to show me and Luke around. He looked at Harvick, looked at me, and gave me a little shake of his head to let me know he thought I'd had much better options available, if only I'd taken him up on his offer.

George and Kerry Matheson were still there, and Matheson asked, "Everything all right now?"

"Fine," I told him. "Just a little misunderstanding."

"There was no misunderstanding about it," Harvick said. "I told a fellow he didn't look anything like Ernest Hemingway, and he didn't."

"I've seen several men in here who look like Hemingway," Kerry said. "I think it's adorable."

Harvick grimaced slightly, but he didn't say anything. I was glad of that. I didn't want him insulting Kerry so that her husband would feel like he had to stick up for her. I could only head off so much trouble in one night.

The bartender handed Harvick his rum punch and collected for it. While Harvick was sipping the drink, a woman came up on his other side and said, "My God, Walter, I heard that you were in a fight. Are you all right?"

"I'm fine," he told her. "It wasn't really much of an altercation."

"Well, thank goodness for that!" she said. "That would be a terrible way to start off a tour, by getting in a brawl!"

I said that Walter Harvick wasn't the sort to attract much attention from women, but maybe I was wrong about that. This one was certainly paying attention to him. She was one of my clients, too. It took me a second to come up with her name: Veronica Scanlon. Ronnie, she had said she preferred to be called.

She was in her thirties and nice-looking, although her lips were a little too thin and her nose a little too sharp for her to be considered pretty. She had long, light brown hair that usually seemed to be a little disheveled. I had no idea what she did for a living. She hadn't volunteered that infor-mation during our brief conversation at the hotel in Miami, before we all boarded the van for Key West. She was one of my singles, though, so I guess it was natural that she might gravitate toward the only eligible man in the bunch. The other two singles were elderly widows originally from New

York who had moved to Florida with their husbands, both of whom had promptly passed away.

"We moved to Florida, we're at least going to see some of the sights," as one of them had told me earlier in the day.

Ronnie Scanlon was still talking to Harvick. I took that as my opportunity to gently disengage from him. I saw a booth open up, grabbed Luke by the arm, and steered him into it before somebody else could get there first.

It was still loud there, but maybe a little less so. Luke and I sat on opposite sides of the booth, and I leaned forward to ask, "You think we can get through the rest of the night and get this bunch back to the hotel without any more trouble?"

"I hope so. People seem to think that just because they're away from home, they can go nuts and act any way they want to."

"That's why folks go on vacation, Luke," I told him. "If they didn't feel that way, we'd be out of business."

"I guess you're right. So what do people like you and me do for vacations?"

"Go home, put our feet up, heave a big sigh of relief, and enjoy the peace and quiet," I said.

It was something to look forward to, and after three days in Key West, I figured I would be ready for it.

Chapter 3

About eleven o'clock, Luke and I left Sloppy Joe's and went back to the parking lot where we'd left the van. I knew from experience that some of the clients might not be the late-night revelers they thought they were. They could have gotten tired and returned to the van early. As soon as everybody showed up, even if it wasn't eleven-thirty yet, we would leave Old Town and head back to the hotel.

When we reached the parking lot, we found Doris Horton and Julia Dunn waiting there for us. Those were the two widowed transplants to Florida.

"That place got too loud for us, Ms. Dickinson," Doris told me. "We did a little window-shopping instead."

"There are a lot of art and antique shops around here," Julia added. "We can come back when they're open, can't we?"

"Of course," I told them. "We'll have some time set aside for shopping each of the next two days, and on the third day you're free to do whatever you like."

"I'm going to spend money, that's what I like," Julia said.

I gave Luke a glance, knowing that he'd understand what I meant by it. You'd like to think that tourist destinations like Key West would be almost free of crime, but that's not always the case. One of Luke's jobs was to keep an eye on some of our older clients who might be more likely to be robbery victims. He gave me a little nod in return, letting me know he knew what I meant.

The Mathesons were the next to arrive, then Phil and Sheila Thompson. Phil taught algebra in a North Carolina high school, while Sheila taught English in the same little town's junior high. They had been saving up for this trip for several years. Phil, stern and crew cut, looked like retired military, which was exactly what he was. Sheila was the Hemingway buff. Phil had come along because he planned to do some deep-sea fishing while they were here and already had trips booked for the next two days. He was going to skip the sightseeing and shopping entirely. On the third day, Luke was taking several of the clients out on a fishing charter while the others had the day free. Phil would be going along on that trip, too. Personally, I couldn't see coming all the way to Key West and spending the whole trip fishing, but that was his decision.

The other two couples, Frank and Jennie Cleburne and Matt and Aimee Altman, showed up a few minutes before eleven-thirty. The Cleburnes were in their thirties, and I didn't know what either of them did for a living. The Altmans were younger, mid-twenties, probably, and from the way they acted, I guessed they hadn't been married for very long. This might have even been their honeymoon, although I didn't get the sense they were quite that newly married. A delayed honeymoon, maybe.

That left Walter Harvick and Ronnie Scanlon. I could see the front of Sloppy Joe's from where we were, and I hadn't noticed either of them coming out of the place while we were waiting. That didn't mean they hadn't slipped out while I wasn't looking, but my hunch was that they were still inside. When it got to be eleven-forty and there was still no sign of them, I told Luke, "I'm gonna go look for them."

"Why don't you just call them?" he asked.

"You heard how much noise there is in there," I said, nodding toward Sloppy Joe's. "They might not hear a phone ring, and if they're in the middle of a crowd, they might not even feel it vibrate."

"I can go look," he offered.

"No, you stay here with the van and our other clients," I told him. "This shouldn't take long."

There was a steady stream of people in and out of the two front doors. A flood of multi-colored neon from the big SLOPPY JOE'S BAR sign on the front of the building washed down over the sidewalk. I walked past the signs promising entertainment, piña coladas, draft beer, and cocktails, past the sign that warned, "Shoes and Shirt Required" – I was all right on both of those scores – and under a painted "Welcome to Sloppy Joe's". The other door had "Hemingway's Favorite Bar" painted on the wall above it. Signs over both doors declared that you had to have a driver's license or state-issued ID to come inside.

I showed the guy at the door my Georgia driver's license and plunged into the crowd again. I got groped a few times, but I told myself it was accidental. The place was so packed that if you actually tried to get fresh with somebody, you might wind up groping something you didn't want to.

There was a tiny open area in front of the bar, though. Not really open, but occupied by only two people: Walter Harvick and Ronnie Scanlon. People were giving them room because they were dancing, the sort of frantic gyrations I hadn't seen since I'd watched a bunch of frugging, boogalooing teenagers on *American Bandstand* when I was a kid.

They seemed to be having fun, so I hated to interrupt them. The rest of my clients were tired and ready to go back to the hotel so they could turn in, though. Matt and Aimee Altman may not have been all that tired, but they were ready to turn in, anyway, if you get my drift.

But I waited until the song was over and Walter and Ronnie almost collapsed in each other's arms. They were both sweaty and out of breath.

"That was great, you two," I said as I moved in, "but we have to go now."

"Already?" Walter asked. "We can get back to the hotel by ourselves, you know. I know the town very well."

"I'm sure you do," I told him, "but since it's our first night in Key West and all, I'd really like to keep everybody together and make sure everything goes smoothly."

"I am kind of tired, Walter," Ronnie said. She smiled. "And a little tipsy, too. I think we should go back."

"Whatever you say," he told her. He put his arm around her shoulders and kissed her on the side of the head. "Whatever my girl wants."

So this was a budding romance now. Well, that was fine. It happened pretty often on tours. Most of them were just quick flings, I suspected, but I like to think that some of them developed into something lasting, although I didn't really know if that had happened on any of my tours.

I took Walter's other arm and maneuvered them toward the exit. Along the way we passed the bouncers who had stepped in earlier during the brief altercation. Walter gave them that smug look, and I'd swear that one of the big bruisers growled at him. Walter just sailed on past, unintimidated. I wanted to tell him not to be a jackass. Pressure points or no pressure points, those bouncers wouldn't have had any trouble tossing him out on his ear.

Walter and Ronnie both swayed a little from too much to drink, but I got them back to the van. Luke helped them in. When he closed the side door, he asked me, "Ready to go?"

"You bet," I told him.

It didn't take long to drive south along Duval to the ocean, although there was still quite a bit of traffic even this late at night. For a small island, Key West seemed to have a lot of cars.

When we reached the Bradenton Beach Resort, I was struck once again by how pretty the place was. Lights burned in a number of the palm trees that were scattered around the property, casting a soft yellow glow over the lawns and flower beds that surrounded the guest cottages.

The centerpiece of the resort was the sprawling, three-story, frame house that had once stood alone on this part of the island, back in the 1840s when the chief industry on Key West had been salvaging cargo from ships that had wrecked on the reefs in the vicinity. In my research on the island I had found out that at one time Key West had a pretty shady reputation, because "wreckers" would use lights to lure ships onto the reefs.

One of those wreckers was an Englishman named Bradenton, who had made a fortune through foul means or fair, and when he turned respectable he had built what was then the finest mansion on Key West, on a large piece of land with a beautiful lawn that sloped gently down to a broad white sandy beach.

Over the years the Bradenton family had fallen on hard times, until in the 1930s, as tourism was starting to boom in the Florida Keys, Claude Bradenton had hit upon the idea of turning the mansion into a hotel and building cottages around it to house even more guests. Since then the Bradentons had lured tourists just like their ancestors had lured ships, only the tourists didn't come to a bad end the way those unfortunate vessels did.

The resort had a pool for those who didn't want to swim in the ocean, a couple of tennis courts, a sauna and a workout room, even a small stable where horses could be rented for sunset rides along the beach. The thing that kept the place from being unaffordable was the age of the main house and the cottages. The rooms were comfortably furnished but a little small, and they lacked some of the luxuries that modern travelers had come to expect, like spa tubs and microwaves and wet bars. Some of the rooms in the main house even shared bathrooms. The atmosphere was quaint and charming, though, and the resort seemed to do plenty of business.

The Mathesons, the Cleburnes, and the Altmans had all opted for cottages, which were more expensive than rooms in the main house. The

Thompsons were staying in the house, as were Walter Harvick, Ronnie Scanlon, Doris Horton, and Julia Dunn. Luke and I each had a room in the house, as well.

Luke parked the van in the gravel lot at the western edge of the property. As everyone climbed out, I reminded them that we would be leaving for the Hemingway House at ten o'clock the next morning. The plan was to take one of the guided tours of the house, then spend the rest of the morning exploring it on our own before having lunch and moving on to the other attractions in Old Town.

The couples staying in cottages scattered along paths paved with crushed shells. The rest of us headed for the main house. The short ride appeared to have sobered up Walter and Ronnie, at least a little. They seemed steadier on their feet, anyway.

The doors to the main house were locked at midnight, I recalled. Guests coming in after that had to be let in by a member of the staff. Someone was on duty all night to handle that, but still it was little annoying. I checked my phone as we went up the steps to the broad verandah that encircled the house. Ten minutes after twelve. We probably would have been there before midnight if I hadn't had to go back into Sloppy Joe's to retrieve Walter and Ronnie, I thought.

There was a button beside the double doors of the main entrance with a sign that said to press it for admittance. Luke did so, and about thirty seconds later a man appeared on the other side of the fancy old doors to unlock them and let us into the small, elegant lobby, which had been formed by knocking out the wall between the foyer and the parlor in the house's original floor plan.

"Evening," the man said as he opened the doors for us. I didn't recall seeing him around the place when we'd checked in earlier. As a member of the resort staff, he wasn't too conscientious about his appearance, either. He was wearing a pair of faded jeans and a pullover shirt with the sleeves cut out of it. And he was barefooted, which took me by surprise. He looked a lot more like a handyman than a concierge or a desk clerk. He went on, "Y'all have fun in town tonight?"

His voice was a soft drawl. I figured he was a Conch (pronounced "Conk", and don't try to say it any other way), somebody who had been born and raised on the island and whose family had probably been here for generations. His arms were muscular and tanned evenly all the way up to his shoulders, telling me it had probably been quite a while since he'd worn a shirt with sleeves in it. His hair was a faded blond, and the effects of sun and wind on his face made it hard to judge his age, but I put him somewhere between forty and fifty.

"Yes, we had a fine time, thanks," I said as I led my clients inside. As they headed for the stairs – there was an elevator, to comply with federal law, but it was small and tucked away, so it was easier to take the stairs – I told them again, "Gather here in the lobby a little before ten tomorrow morning."

I got waves of acknowledgment from Doris and Julia, and from Sheila Thompson as well. Walter had his arm around Ronnie's waist, and she was giggling. Those two were only going to need one room tonight, I thought, and I didn't know whether to think more power to 'em or hope that it wouldn't complicate things and lead to trouble.

"You sound like you're the mother hen to this

bunch of chicks," the man who had let us in said.

"I'm in charge of the tour," I told him, pausing at the bottom of the stairs with Luke while the others all went up to their rooms.

"That would make you Delilah Dickinson," he said. I was a little surprised he knew my name.

"That's right. This is my associate, Luke Edwards." I usually didn't mention that Luke was also my son-in-law. He preferred it that way. I don't think he wanted folks to know that he worked for his mother-in-law.

The man put out his hand to me and said, "Pleased to meet y'all. My name's Tom Bradenton. I sort of own the place."

Chapter 4

Well, that explained how he could dress like a beach bum and still work here, I thought as I shook hands with him. "It's nice to meet you," I told him. "The resort is just lovely."

"Thanks, I like it here, too." He turned to Luke and shook hands with him. "Hey, Luke, how you doin'?"

"All right, I guess," Luke said. "We've been wrangling tourists all evening."

"Yeah, it can get crazy in Old Town, can't it? To be honest, I don't go down there that much. After growing up here, you feel like you've seen it all before. I stay pretty close to home."

I'd heard similar sentiments expressed by people who lived in areas that drew a lot of tourists. They tended to keep a low profile and just go on about their business.

"So if you folks need anything, just let me know," Tom Bradenton continued. "I'm usually around."

"We appreciate that, Mr. Bradenton," I said.

He flashed a grin at me. "Tom," he said. "Mr. Bradenton – "

"Was your father," I finished for him.

"That's right. Well, good night," he added as he turned toward a small room just off the lobby. The door was open, and from the glimpse I got inside, the room was an office, although a fairly cluttered and informal one. That seemed to fit Tom Bradenton's personality.

Luke and I went upstairs to our rooms. The second floor corridor was dimly lit. There weren't any fluorescent lights, just regular bulbs in old-fashioned wall sconces. It was a nice, quaint touch that fit in with the rest of the place.

So was the elegant four-poster bed in my room and the gleaming hardwood dresser and chest. The bathroom was small, with most of the space taken up by a claw-footed bathtub. I had a nice soak in it, then climbed into bed and slept well. The trip down here and the evening at Sloppy Joe's had worn me out.

* * *

The resort provided a continental breakfast in the dining room of the main house. I sampled the pecan pancakes and found them to be delicious. Luke went for the beer-battered version and pronounced them wonderful. The coffee was excellent, too. Tom Brandenton put on a good spread.

Luke and I were there at nine o'clock. During the next hour, most of the members of our tour wandered in to eat before setting out on the day's activities.

Sheila Thompson was by herself. Her husband Phil, she explained to me, had been up well before the crack of dawn and by now would be miles out in the Atlantic on a charter boat, deep-sea fishing. I couldn't imagine why anybody would want to do that – I can get seasick on a mile-long ferry ride – but since that was how Phil preferred to spend his time, it was fine with me.

Matt and Aimee Altman were yawning, a not surprising indication that they hadn't gotten much sleep. The others all seemed a little brighter-eyed. The only ones who hadn't shown up by nine-forty-five were Walter Harvick and Ronnie Scanlon. I didn't want to have to go hunt them down, so I hoped they would put in an appearance soon.

Everyone was finished with breakfast and had drifted back out into the lobby by ten. Footsteps on the stairs made me look up. Walter was coming down by himself. I met him at the bottom of the staircase and said, "Mornin', Mr. Harvick. How are you?"

"Fine," he said. "Ready to visit the Hemingway House. By the way, if you need any help pointing out or explaining things, just let me know. I've been there many times."

"I think I can manage, thanks," I said, trying not to let him see my irritation. It was true that he probably knew a lot more about Hemingway than I did, but this was my tour, doggone it. I'd been in this business long enough to know that buffs of any sort can be the bane of a tour director. "You're a little too late for breakfast."

"That's all right. I had coffee in my room. That's all I need."

"What about Ms. Scanlon?"

He frowned. "What about her?"

"Well, I sort of thought the two of you would be together . . ."

My voice trailed off as he frowned at me. Looked like I had sort of stepped in it, unintentionally. The way they'd been carrying on with each other in

Sloppy Joe's and on the way back here, I'd just assumed they would be spending the rest of the night together.

But even if they had, I reminded myself, Ronnie could have gone back to her room early this morning, or Walter back to his, depending on where they'd stayed. I'd jumped the gun by assuming they'd come down together.

"I see," Walter said coolly. "You thought that because we were both a bit under the influence last night, there was some sort of illicit romance going on."

I tried to repair the damage by saying, "There's nothing illicit about a couple of folks enjoyin' each other's company – "

More footsteps made me glance up. Ronnie Scanlon was coming down the stairs, and the look she gave Walter was downright icy, especially considering the fact that Key West had never experienced a frost, as far as anyone knew.

Trouble in Paradise, I thought. Something had happened between these two, and it hadn't been good.

"Good morning, Ms. Dickinson," Ronnie greeted me. She looked narrow-eyed at Walter and added, "Mr. Harvick."

"Ms. Scanlon," he said, every bit as cold and unfriendly as she was.

I wasn't sure what held the most potential for trouble, a romance between these two or the falling-out that had obviously taken place. None of it was my business, though. We were here to see the sights, starting with the Hemingway House, and that was what we were going to do.

"Come on everybody," I said as I turned toward the door. "Let's get started."

I led the way with Luke bringing up the rear to corral any stragglers. I was wearing sandals, slacks, and a sleeveless lime green blouse. Luke had opted for shorts and a t-shirt, and the clients were all dressed very casually as well, with the younger women showing quite a bit of skin. You didn't have to be on Key West for very long before a tendency toward informality kicked in.

As we headed for the parking lot I saw Tom Bradenton coming toward us. He wore cut-off jeans and a t-shirt and was wet from head to foot, having just come out of the ocean from a morning swim, I thought. "Mornin', y'all," he said with a wave as we went past him.

"Is that the handyman who let us in last night?" Doris Horton asked me.

"He's very handsome," Julia Dunn said, "and I think he was smiling at you, Ms. Dickinson."

"Oh, I think he's just friendly," I said without explaining who Tom really was. "He was smilin' at all of us."

I wasn't sure that was completely true, though. There had seemed to be a little extra warmth in Tom's eyes as he looked at me.

Not that it mattered. We were only going to be there for three days.

Luke and I got everybody loaded onto the van and started on the short drive across the island. I'd been to Key West before, as a tourist myself, so I knew that street parking was a problem in most places around Old Town. I'd made an arrangement with one of the off-street lots to hold a place for us. That meant a little more expense and walking, but luckily Key West was small. We were only a few blocks from the Hemingway House, at Whitehead and Olivia, when we climbed out of the van.

Ronnie Scanlon had stopped shooting venomous looks at Walter. Now she was just ignoring him. That was an improvement as far as I was concerned.

The house that Ernest and Pauline Hemingway bought and remodeled in 1931 is a sprawling, two-story structure built of limestone blocks quarried on-site. It has tall windows flanked by greenish-yellow shutters, and verandahs wrap all the way around both floors, the upper one forming a balcony enclosed by a wrought-iron railing. A large yard with flower beds and palm trees surrounds the house.

The whole house is open to the public except for Hemingway's writing room, which is upstairs above an old carriage house in the back of the property. Tourists can look into that room, where he wrote parts of several novels and a number of short stories, through a screen but can't go in.

A small, white-framed ticket booth with the same sort of shuttered windows sits out front. I'd already paid the admission fee for the entire group, so we didn't have to stand in line to get in. I did, however, point out the sign displayed prominently next to the ticket window: PLEASE DO NOT PICK UP CATS.

"The famous six-toed cats?" Kerry Matheson asked.

"That's right," I told her. "Descended from the ones that lived here when Hemingway did."

Walter said, "Actually, some of them have seven or eight toes. They're quite unusual looking."

"And they run free," I added. "Just don't pick 'em up, like the sign says."

We moved on to the first floor verandah and walked all the way around the house first, getting a good view of the grounds. Pauline Hemingway had put in a swimming pool, quite an extravagance for the time. The water was rather greenish at the moment and didn't look too attractive to me. I figured that with the year-round heat, it would be pretty hard to maintain a pool. The algae had to love it here in Key West.

The heat was worse inside, without much air stirring despite a number of open windows and doors. Walter pointed to one of the fancy chandeliers and said, "The house had ceiling fans when the Hemingways bought it, but Pauline had them taken out and replaced with these chandeliers."

"Not smart," Frank Cleburne said. He had taken a handkerchief from the back pocket of his shorts and used it to mop sweat from his forehead. "Actually what the place could use is a good central AC unit."

Walter looked at him with something like horror and said, "That would violate the historical accuracy of the site."

"Yeah, but it'd be a lot cooler."

Walter shook his head as if he couldn't even begin to comprehend that attitude. Frank looked a little annoyed by Walter's reaction, but his wife Jennie touched him on the arm and steered him into one of the other rooms.

I'd been here before, but it had been a number of years earlier. I hadn't forgotten how the cats were all over the place, though. Tabbies, calicos, longhairs and short, all of them so used to strangers trooping around that they paid little attention to the tourists. Of course, cats don't really get worked up much about humans to start with. I think they consider us a lower form of life to be tolerated as long as we behave ourselves. Not all of them had six or more toes, either. Some of them were just plain ol' alley cats. They would put up with being petted, but that was about it.

"They're so sweet," Aimee Altman said. She slid her hand under the belly of a big orange tabby, but her husband Matt stopped her.

"Remember, we're not supposed to pick them up," he told her.

"What would it hurt?"

"I imagine that's the owners' way of saying that if you get clawed it's not their fault, and you can't sue them."

"More than likely," I agreed with him. "Anyway, we'd better follow the rules."

Aimee shrugged and let go of the tabby. She was darned cute, with a heart-shaped face, long blond hair so pale it was almost white, and the sort of body that twenty-year-olds don't think anything about. It never occurs to them that in another fifteen or twenty years, they'll have to work really, really hard to look half that good. Matt absolutely adored her, you could tell that just by looking at him.

The house is simply but comfortably furnished with heavy Spanish-style furniture, much of which actually had belonged to the Hemingways, and you can tell it would have been a nice place to live. Other than the fact that Ernest Hemingway lived here, though, there isn't really anything that distinctive about it. It's just a nice old house.

After touring both floors, we left through a side door and crossed the yard to the squarish, two-story outbuilding where Hemingway's studio was located. An outside staircase led up to the second floor. Walter pointed up to the second-floor balcony of the main house and said, "When Hemingway lived here, he had a gate cut in the railing and a rope bridge strung from the balcony over to the other building so he could get to his studio without having to go downstairs."

Luke leaned over to me and whispered, "Did you know that?"

"As a matter of fact, I did," I answered with a slight frown. I prided myself on doing my home-work before I led these tours, and here Walter was stepping all over the things I had learned.

You don't last long in business by fussing at your customers, though, so I didn't say anything to him. Let him show off all he wanted to. It wasn't having any effect on Ronnie Scanlon, who alter-nated between ignoring him and glaring at him. Whatever had happened between them, she seemed to be determined not to let him ruin her trip for her . . . but he was coming close to it anyway.

We went upstairs to look at the writing room. The screened-off door was small enough that only a couple of people could look at a time. The room was spacious and bright, with windows on opposite walls and two French doors in a third wall that let in plenty of light. A small round table with a typewriter on it sat in the center of the room with a plain, straight-backed chair in front of it. Short bookshelves were arranged around the walls, and above the bookshelf between the French doors was the mounted head of an antelope – or some animal like that, I'm not any sort of hunter – one of Hemingway's trophies. A mounted fish hung on the same wall, off to the side, and there were framed portraits of Hemingway from different times in his life, too.

It probably hadn't looked much like this when

he was here, I thought. Back then it had been a place for him to work; now it was a museum. I could imagine the desk with stacks of paper around the typewriter and a pencil lying here and there. I could see Hemingway sitting there, blunt fingers pounding the keys or holding one of the pencils as he made corrections on a manuscript. I wouldn't be leading these literary tours if something about the whole process of writing didn't strike me as almost magical and very appealing.

"What did he write here?" Doris Horton asked.

As I was coming to expect, Walter was quick with the answer and beat me to it. "Parts of *Death in the Afternoon*, *The Green Hills of Africa*, *To Have and Have Not*, and *For Whom the Bell Tolls*. And some short stories as well, like 'The Snows of Kilimanjaro'. Hemingway never stayed still for too long at a time, so it was unusual for him to start and finish a project in the same place. Even though this was his main residence for almost a decade, he was always jaunting off to Paris or New York or Idaho or Cuba. Quite a life, don't you think?"

"I don't know," Julia Dunn said. "I think I'd get tired of traveling around all the time. I don't mind sightseeing like this, but when I'm done I want to go home."

"Ah, but that misses all the romance of being a writer," Walter said.

"As if you'd know anything about romance," Ronnie muttered. If Walter heard her, he didn't show any sign of it.

Somebody was sure disappointed, I thought, but then I steered my mind quickly away from that.

It never hurts to get to know your clients, but some things you're just better off not knowing.

Chapter 5

Downstairs in the old carriage house was the museum bookstore and gift shop. I turned the members of the group loose to browse down there or wander around the grounds and look at things on their own.

Matt and Aimee headed off into the gardens right away, hand in hand. I figured they planned to find a hidden spot for some smooching. Kerry, Sheila, Jennie, Doris, and Julia formed another group and focused their attention on the gift shop. That left George and Frank on their own. They stuck their hands in their pockets and made some awkward small talk. Wives always bond on these trips better than husbands do.

I figured out why Frank had made that comment about central air conditioning units. Turned out he sold and installed them, back in Oklahoma. That meant George had to tell Frank about his plumbing supply business in Kentucky.

I looked around for Walter and Ronnie but didn't see them anywhere. Luke was hunkered down on one of the patios, petting a longhaired black and white cat that seemed to really be enjoying it. Out of curiosity, I counted the toes. The front paws were normal, but the cat had six toes on its hind feet.

"Hey, Luke," I said. "Come over here a minute, will you?"

He gave the cat's ears a last scratch and said, "See you later, buddy." Then he stood up and came over to me. "What's up, Miz D?"

"We seem to be missin' a couple of clients."

He grinned. "You mean the Altmans? I'm sure they're around somewhere." His voice lowered to a conspiratorial tone. "I think they're honeymooners."

"Yeah, I got that idea. I was talking about Mr. Harvick and Ms. Scanlon."

Luke looked around and frowned. "They're probably in the house. He's kind of a show-off. Probably trying to impress her with all he knows about Hemingway."

"Maybe." I had a bad feeling crawling around in the back of my mind anyway. We'd run into trouble on previous tours, and clearly there was some hostility between those two. As annoying as Walter was, I didn't want Ronnie trying to choke him to death. "You stay here in case anybody needs anything. I'm gonna go see if I can find them."

"Would you like me to do that?"

"No, I've got it," I told him. Back there in that nervous part of my brain, I was thinking that if anybody was going to stumble over a dead body, it ought to be me, not Luke. At least I had some experience along those lines.

There was no need to be nervous, I told myself as I started walking around the grounds of the estate. Absolutely no reason to think that anything bad might have happened. What was in the past was in the past. I went down a curving path that led between some palm trees and by some thick shrubbery. No way was I going to see the legs of a corpse sticking out of those bushes, I thought.

And I was right. No legs, arms, or any other part of a dead body.

But I did hear a feminine giggle coming from back there in the vegetation.

That would be Matt and Aimee Altman, I guessed. They'd found themselves a nice romantic spot for some canoodling. I was happy for them, but that didn't help me find Walter and Ronnie. They might still be at each other's throat for all I knew.

Then I heard a voice that didn't belong to Aimee saying, "Oh, Walter, I'm so glad we worked things out. I knew it couldn't end like that."

Well, well. So Walter and Ronnie had made up after all. I still didn't know what had happened between them the night before, didn't want to know. It was enough that she wouldn't be glaring at him for the rest of the trip and he wouldn't be acting supercilious toward her. I hoped.

I turned around to make my way back to the house. I didn't want to intrude on the reconciliation that was going on in the shrubbery. A big yellow tabby started pacing along beside me on the walk.

When I reached the verandah, Luke was there talking fishing with Frank and George. They would be headed out on the charter boat in a couple of days, along with Phil Thompson, of course. Jennie was going along, too; according to Frank she enjoyed deep-sea fishing. She was the only one of the women who planned to make the trip.

I poked my head into the bookstore and gift shop. The ladies still seemed to be enjoying themselves, so I didn't interrupt. My itinerary called for us to stay here at the Hemingway House until twelve-thirty or so, then head deeper into Old Town for lunch and a little more shopping, then take the Conch Tour Train which would give the tourists a good overview of the entire island.

Since everything seemed to be under control for the moment, I figured it was a good time for me to relax a little. I found a wicker chair on the verandah and sat down. I hadn't been there more than a minute when the big yellow tabby that had been following me around earlier sauntered up and jumped into my lap.

"Well, hello," I said. He turned around, and his long, fuzzy tail brushed across my face. I was glad I wasn't allergic to cats, or I would have been sneezing by then. Since the cat was in my lap, demanding attention, I rubbed his ears.

Matt and Aimee came around the corner of the house, and when Aimee saw me she said, "Hey, no fair! I didn't get to play with the kitties."

"It was his idea, not mine," I said. "You're right, though, I wouldn't want to get in trouble." I took hold of the cat and set him on the ground. "Go ahead, shoo."

He looked up at me like was mortally offended, then after a second stalked off, tail held high.

I stood up and said to the young couple, "Y'all havin' a good time so far?"

"It's been wonderful," Aimee said. "Key West is so . . . so picturesque!"

"And hot," Matt added. He wiped sweat off his forehead. Actually, both of them were pretty red-faced, and I thought once again that they'd probably been making out. Youth isn't always wasted on the young.

And speaking of making out . . . Walter and Ronnie came up the walk from the gardens, smiling and holding hands now. That was a complete turnaround from the way they'd been acting earlier.

Matt noticed that, too, raising an eyebrow in surprise. "Hey, Walter," he said. "You want to tell us some more about Hemingway?"

"Of course," Walter said, apparently not realizing that Matt was teasing him a little. Beside Matt, Aimee hung on to his arm and stifled a giggle. Walter went on, "What do you want to know?"

"Well, ol' Ernest was sort of a player, wasn't he?"

Walter shook his head. "I don't know what you mean."

"Didn't he have a girlfriend in Paris while he and his wife were living here in Key West? I think I read something about that."

"Oh, you mean Martha Gellhorn. Well, it's true that he was carrying on with Martha while he was still married to Pauline. But he was a great artist, and they don't really have to follow the same rules as the rest of us. Hemingway had to follow his muse."

"Sounds like he was following something else," Matt said with a grin.

Aimee laughed and said, "You're terrible."

"No, I'm thinking of becoming a writer. That way I can have me a girlfriend on the side, too."

Aimee punched him on the arm, but she was still laughing. "Now you really *are* terrible!"

Walter frowned and said, "Wait a minute. Are you making fun of Hemingway?"

"Aw, not really," Matt said. "It's just that the whole thing . . . well, it's kind of a joke, isn't it? Big, tough writer, the whole manly man thing, and he picks on people and cheats on his wife and takes himself so dang seriously . . . I mean, you've got to admit, by this time it's all sort of a joke."

"A joke," Walter repeated, and I didn't like the way his face was getting red as he said it. "If you think Hemingway was a joke, then why are you even here?"

Ronnie put a hand on his arm and said, "Now, Walter, don't get all worked up."

He shook her off and took a step toward Matt. "Really," he went on, "why did you even bother?"

"Hey, take it easy, man. I didn't mean to offend you. I mean, I know ol' Ernie's your guy. Aimee and me, we mainly came for the resort, but we thought we'd take in some of the sights while we're here, too."

"You shouldn't make fun of things you don't understand. Things that you're not smart enough to understand."

Matt frowned and said, "Hey."

"Walter, please – " Ronnie began.

Aimee was getting mad, too. She said, "You can't talk to my husband like that."

Matt was a good ten years younger, about the same height as Walter, but a lot more athletic. You wouldn't think he'd have any trouble handling somebody like Walter in a fight, but I remembered what Walter had done to that Hemingway lookalike in Sloppy Joe's the night before.

Anyway, I didn't want a fight on one of my tours. I moved quickly and got between them, making my voice firm yet friendly as I said, "Hey, folks, it's too hot here for anybody to get all worked up. Why don't we just call a truce? Aimee, have you been to the gift shop yet?"

She was still glaring at Walter, but she took the

opportunity for a way out of this confrontation. She said, "No, I haven't," and tugged at Matt's arm. "Come on. I want to take a look in there."

"Okay, okay." He let her turn him away from Walter. They headed toward the gift shop, and that probably would have been the end of it if Matt hadn't said loud enough for the rest of us to hear him, "Big tough guy and he does a gutless thing like blowing his head off with a shotgun. Big ol' coward's more like it."

Walter started after him, and from the look on his face I knew there was going to be trouble. I grabbed one arm, and Ronnie grabbed the other.

"Wait, Walter, please don't," she said.

We managed to stop him. We hung on to him until Matt and Aimee disappeared into the gift shop. Then we let go and he sort of shook loose from us at the same time. He glared at me, but he said, "I don't blame you for interceding, Ms. Dickinson. Naturally you don't want trouble on one of your tours." The look he gave Ronnie was even angrier as he went on, "But you . . . don't ever interfere with me again."

She blinked, clearly hurt. "But Walter," she said, "I . . . I was just trying to help – "

"I don't need your help," he snapped. He stalked off, and since he was heading toward the front of the estate, away from the gift shop where Matt was, I let him go without trying to stop him.

Ronnie stared after him, her face a mixture of surprise and resentment, and after a moment she burst out, "That *ass hat!*"

That was a pretty good description of Walter Harvick, I thought.

"I'm sorry that happened, Ms. Scanlon . . . Ronnie," I said. "Walter seems a mite . . . high-strung."

"That's putting it mildly," she said, still glowering. "Last night at the resort, after we . . . after . . . well, he practically kicked me out of his room. He said that we were done, that he didn't have time for anything as . . . as trivial as any sort of relationship with me! He was here on important business, he said, not just to get . . . well . . ."

I held my hands up to stop her. I'd already heard more than I really wanted to.

"Sometimes it's hard to figure out what a fella really wants," I said. "Most of the time they don't know themselves."

"Oh, he knows. He won't talk about it, but he knows. And that doesn't make him any less of an ass hat."

She was right about that, too.

I was trying to figure out what to tell her to make her feel better about things, when around at the front of the house, somebody started yelling. Two somebodies, in fact.

And my heart sank when I realized that one of them was Walter Harvick.

Chapter 6

"Now what?" I muttered to myself as I took off around the house in a hurry. Ronnie trotted along beside me.

"He's gotten somebody else mad at him," she said. "He can be so nice, and then he's just mean."

From what I had seen so far, that summed up Walter, all right.

As we came around the corner, I spotted Walter standing on the verandah with a big, white-bearded man. They were jawing at each other with such ferocity that the other tourists scattered around the yard were regarding them nervously.

I recognized the large bearded man as the Hemingway lookalike Walter had clashed with at Sloppy Joe's. I didn't know what he was doing here, but I wasn't really surprised to see him. Big, white-bearded guys in fishing caps were all over Key West. This one also wore cargo shorts and a brightly flowered shirt.

"I just don't understand why they would hire a fraud like you," Walter was saying as Ronnie and I approached.

"I'm not a fraud, blast it," the other man thundered right back at him. "I look just like Hemingway, and I know more about him than you do!"

I knew that was a challenge that Walter would never let pass, and sure enough he shouted back, "I've forgotten more about Hemingway than you'll ever know! I even know what happened on Bedford Key!"

That seemed to throw the bearded man for a loop. He frowned and said, "I never even heard of – "

"Ah-ha!" Walter crowed. "You see what I'm talking about!"

"Walter," Ronnie began, but then she stopped. Maybe she was remembering how he'd spoken to her just a few minutes earlier.

I pressed on. "Walter, you don't want to waste your time here arguin'," I said. "Come on, you can show me around. I'll listen to whatever you want to tell me."

Walter flapped a dismissive hand at the bearded man and said with a sneer, "Why don't you let this so-called tour guide show you around?"

Well, that explained what the bearded man was doing here, anyway. I knew that the Hemingway House had a number of different tour guides, and it didn't surprise me that at least one of them came from the hordes of would-be Hemingways.

"I'm fully qualified – " this one started to say.

"Yes, to be a beach bum," Walter interrupted.

"All right, that's enough," I said, and I was prétty mad myself by now. "Walter, you come with me."

"You can't tell me what to do," he objected.

"I'll refund your money and you can get back to Miami on your own if you don't behave yourself," I said, and right then, I meant every word of it, although the concept of refunding money definitely went against the grain.

I thought he was going to argue with me, but then he shrugged.

"Grace under pressure," he said.

"That's right. Now come on."

I took his arm and led him away from the bearded man. Rollie, that was the fella's name. I remembered it now from what the bouncers in Sloppy Joe's had said.

Ronnie tagged along, looking nervous and irritated at the same time, as I led Walter over to a wrought iron bench and sat him down. I motioned for Ronnie to sit down beside him and said, "Now, the two of you talk about something pleasant. You got that, Walter? No bein' a jerk."

"You think I'm a jerk?" He sounded genuinely surprised.

"I think you're actin' like one part of the time. Now be nice."

"Okay, okay," he muttered as he looked down at the flagstone walk. I couldn't tell if he genuinely chastened or not, but I was going to hope.

I pointed a finger at Walter, then moved it back and forth between him and Ronnie. "You two gonna be all right?"

"Yeah, sure." He even looked over at Ronnie and went on, "I'm sorry. I guess I, uh, don't really know how to act around women."

That was an understatement, I thought.

Ronnie was more inclined to forgiveness, though. She said, "That's all right, Walter. As long as you do like Ms. Dickinson says and behave yourself, we'll be fine."

He nodded and even summoned up a smile.

"Thanks."

With the two of them seemingly settled on the bench for a while, I told them we'd be leaving for lunch in Old Town in another half-hour or so, then went looking for the bearded man. I found him inside the house, talking to one of the other tour guides. I heard enough to know that he was complaining about Walter.

When he turned to me, I said, "I'm sorry, Mister . . .?"

"Cranston," he said. "Rollie Cranston. I remember you from last night in Sloppy Joes." He might still be mad at Walter, but he gave me a grin anyway. "I never forget a good-looking redhead."

"Well, I appreciate that, but I wanted to apologize on behalf of my client. I'm the director of the tour that Walter belongs to."

"I'll bet that guy didn't send you in here, did he?" Cranston asked. "I know the type. Never wrong about anything. Can't even conceive of it."

"Well . . ."

"Don't worry about it," he said with a wave of a big hand. "I've dealt with visitors like him before. We get lots of Hemingway buffs here."

"I'll bet you do," I told him. "I'm glad you're takin' it so well."

"We're paid to get along with the tourists." He grinned again. "But if you really want to make it up to me, I'm in Sloppy Joe's 'most every night. You could stop by and have a drink with me. I'd consider it square if you'd do that. We'd call the whole matter closed."

I stopped wearing my wedding ring when I got divorced, so by now I was used to middle-aged guys hitting on me. Most of the time I didn't take offense at it. Sometimes I even liked it. But Rollie Cranston wasn't my type.

Still, he was just talking about one drink in a crowded nightspot. What could it hurt?

"Sure," I said.

* * *

After chatting with Rollie for a few more minutes, I went to start rounding up the members of the group. Ronnie was still sitting with Walter on the bench. Walter looked like he had calmed down considerably. The other women, along with Matt Altman, were still in the gift shop, and I found Luke, George Matheson, and Frank Cleburne standing by the swimming pool discussing pool filters. Feeling a little like I was herding a flock of chickens, I gathered them up and herded them away from the Hemingway House and back toward the center of Old Town.

There were plenty of places to eat, ranging from national chains like the Hard Rock Café to obscure little hole-in-the-wall diners. I'd gotten a recommendation for a restaurant called The Red Top, for its Spanish-style red tile roof, and found it without much trouble. It was busy but not packed, which told me that the food was good but that so far it had escaped becoming trendy. Most of the customers, in fact, looked more like locals than tourists.

"All right, we're all gonna be on our best be-havior," I told the group as we paused just inside the door.

"Was that directed at me?" Walter asked.

"Nope, I'm not singlin' out anybody," I told him . . . although to be honest, I probably was more worried about him than any of the others. If

Matt wanted to take it as a hint not to tease Walter anymore, though, that was fine with me.

The cuisine was Cuban, mostly beef and assorted seafood dishes, served with black beans and rice, and I thought it was very good. Everybody else seemed to think so as well. I got the impression that everybody was pleasantly stuffed as we left.

After eating that much, it felt good to walk. We strolled up Duval, taking in all the colorful shops and businesses and the even more colorful swarms of people. The sidewalks got even more crowded when we reached Front Street, near Mallory Square where all the cruise ships docked. That was where we caught the Conch Tour Train.

Despite its name, it wasn't really a train. The "engine" that pulled the open cars with bench seats was made to look like a locomotive but actually ran on tires, as did the passenger cars. From it we got good looks at the waterfront, the Harry Truman House, the Key West Lighthouse, the Flagler Railroad Museum, the fascinating architecture of the old houses, and some of the most beautiful beaches in the world. The next day we would be taking the Key West Trolley Tour, which would allow us to get on and off and explore those sights at our leisure. The trip on the Conch Train was more just to get everybody oriented. I didn't want anybody getting separated from the group and getting lost, although Key West was small enough that I didn't think it would be that hard to find them again.

After we got off the Conch Train at the Front Street station, I told everyone, "We'll walk back to the van now and head for the resort. You've gotten a good look at the island, so you'll be on your own for the rest of the afternoon and for supper tonight.

I'm told that the resort has an excellent dining room, but there are also regular shuttles from there to Old Town, so if you want to try one of the restaurants or cafés we saw today, that's fine, too. You might also want to take in the sunset celebration in Mallory Square. There's always a lot going on there."

I got a few nods, but not very enthusiastic ones. We had walked enough so that everybody was a little tired and sweaty. We had reached the time of day when, in this climate, folks wanted to take a nice cool shower and then stretch out for a nap before the evening's festivities. To tell you the truth, that sounded pretty darned good to me, too.

Walter Harvick had been on his best behavior during the afternoon. I noticed that he and Matt stayed as far apart as they could, and we didn't run into anybody else Walter could argue with. That was a relief.

The trip back to the Bradenton Beach Resort was uneventful. When we got there, everyone headed for their rooms. I would have, too, but Tom Bradenton came into the lobby just as I was about to go up the stairs. He smiled at me, and I paused.

"How was your day, Ms. Dickinson?" he asked.

"Delilah," I reminded him. He was a little more formally dressed now, which meant he had on jeans and a polo shirt and had on sandals instead of being barefoot. He still didn't look like a guy who owned a luxury resort.

"Well, then, Delilah," he said, "did your group have fun today?"

"Yeah, for the most part, I think they did."

"Uh-oh," he said, his smile disappearing. "What does that 'for the most part' mean?"

I hesitated before answering. I like to keep what

happens on a tour private. The old "what happens in Vegas" concept. But Tom was so blasted likeable and seemed genuinely concerned, so I said, "One of my clients seems to have a habit of rubbing people the wrong way. Nothing major, you understand, just a little irritating."

Tom nodded and said, "Mr. Harvick."

"How did you know?" I asked, surprised.

"He gave housekeeping a little trouble when he arrived yesterday. Didn't think the room had been cleaned quite well enough. And early this morning he decided he didn't have enough towels."

"I didn't know anything about that," I told Tom with a shake of my head. "I'm sorry."

He waved that off. "Oh, it's nothing to worry about. We're pretty used to guests being picky. Mr. Harvick's not any worse than a lot of others. You know how it is in the hospitality business, you try to make people happy. Some of them are easier to please than others."

"Yeah, of course."

"Maybe he has that, what do you call it, Asperger's Syndrome."

"No," I said, "I think he's just an ass hat. That's what his girlfriend called him."

Tom quirked an eyebrow at me. "Girlfriend?" he repeated. "I didn't realize one of the ladies was traveling with him."

"Well, it didn't start out that way. Just a little tour fling, I think. I shouldn't say any more."

His grin came back. "I understand. That's something else about the hospitality business . . . the need for discretion."

"Amen."

"So, what are your plans for this evening?"

I suddenly wondered if Tom Bradenton wanted

to ask me out. Maybe he was interested in a little tour fling. Or maybe he actually liked me. Unfortunately I'd promised Rollie Cranston that I'd have a drink with him at Sloppy Joe's.

"I've, uh, got a date. Sort of."

"Oh." Tom didn't stop smiling, but he looked a little disappointed.

"It's nothing serious, I just promised to have a drink with somebody. I'll probably be back here pretty early."

"All right. Maybe I'll see you then, if I'm around." He paused. "And I'm usually around."

We said our goodbyes and I headed upstairs, wondering if I was making a big mistake by not blowing off that drink with Rollie Cranston. Nothing was going to come of it, I knew that, but I was a whole lot less certain of what the prospects of spending more time with Tom might lead to.

But I'd given Rollie my word, and I like to keep my promises.

Besides, we were going to be here for a couple more days. There was still time to get to know Tom Bradenton a little better.

Chapter 7

The shower and the nap made me feel better, as I knew they would. I was considerably refreshed when I went downstairs for supper in the dining room in the main house. I'd already made arrangements to eat with Luke.

"How's Melissa doing?" I asked him as we sat down at one of the tables covered with a white linen cloth. The dining room wasn't very big, only a dozen tables, a couple of them long enough to accommodate larger parties.

"She's fine," he said. "A little jealous, I think, that I got to come down here and she didn't."

"That's what she gets for bein' so dang good at runnin' the office," I told him with a smile. "Really, though, you ought to consider bringin' her back for a vacation, just the two of you, now that you know your way around the place."

"You think she'd like that?"

"I know she would."

My daughter had been really tolerant about staying home and keeping the business running smoothly while Luke was off gallivanting around on tours with me. Melissa deserved a getaway of her own.

"But how would you get by without both of us around?" Luke asked, apparently in all seriousness.

"I *am* a grown woman, you know," I said. "And I've run travel agency offices before. Next time we've got a couple of weeks with no tours, the two of you should just take off. Come back here to Key West, or go anywhere else you want. Consider it a second honeymoon."

"That sounds really good," he said, nodding.

"And who knows?" I went on. "Maybe I'll even get a grandbaby out of the deal."

That made him turn red, as I knew it would. He started hemming and hawing around, and I took pity on him and reached across the table to pat his hand and shut him up.

"Don't worry about it, honey," I said. "I'm just jokin'." Then I added, "Sort of."

The waitress came over then to take our orders, and Luke looked mightily relieved at the interruption.

Luke opted for steak, but I knew the fish in the Keys was always fresh and good, so I had the grilled mahi mahi. I thought Tom Bradenton might wander into the dining room and say hello, but there was no sign of him so I had to settle for a delicious meal, and that was fine with me.

Doris Horton and Julia Dunn ate in the dining room, too, as did the Cleburnes. They paused by our table as they came in, and Jennie said, "I think we'll just stay in tonight if that's all right. We're not as young as we used to be."

"That's fine," I told her, but Doris spoke up from the next table, saying, "Not as young as you used to be? Why, that's nonsense. You're both practically children."

"Tell that to my sore muscles," Frank said. "I guess I'm not used to walking as much as we did today."

"We're not going back out, either," Julia said. "I'm afraid the nightlife here is a little too rowdy for a couple of old ladies."

Doris snorted and said, "Speak for yourself. I could hold my own with those kids . . . if I wanted to."

Somehow, I didn't really doubt that.

After supper, as Luke and I went out into the lobby, Ronnie Scanlon came up to us with a slightly worried look on her face.

"Have either of you seen Walter?" she asked. "I thought we'd go back to Duval Street tonight, but he's not in his room and I can't find him anywhere else around here. I tried calling him, but he's not answering his cell phone."

I shook my head and said, "Sorry. Haven't seen him since he went upstairs earlier. Did y'all make definite plans to get together?"

"Well, no," Ronnie admitted. "I said I'd like to, and he didn't say he was opposed to the idea . . . Maybe I should have pinned him down on it, instead of just assuming that he agreed with me."

Walter struck me as the sort who needed to be pinned down, all right, otherwise he was liable to go off on any sort of tangent. If Ronnie had been counting on his company tonight, she might well be disappointed.

"I'll look around for him if you want," Luke offered.

"Would you?" Ronnie said. "That would be great. Thank you, Mr. Edwards."

"Shoot, call me Luke. Everybody does." He looked at me. "What about you, Miz D?"

"I'm supposed to meet somebody," I said.

His eyebrows went up. "Oh? Anybody special?"

"You know better than that," I told him. "And there's no hurry. I'll help look for Walter, too."

If Rollie Cranston got tired of waiting for me at Sloppy Joe's and took off, that would just be too bad, I thought. I hadn't made any firm promises.

I went on, "Maybe we'd better check his room again first, and if he's not there, we can split up and look around the resort for him."

Ronnie nodded, still looking distracted by worry.

Walter didn't answer Luke's knock on his door. Luke looked at me and asked, "You want me to try the knob?"

I didn't know what to say. Once again those memories of the bad things that had happened on some of my other tours floated to the top of my thoughts. I couldn't help but consider the possibility that Walter Harvick was inside his room, all right . . . dead.

That seemed pretty far-fetched, but I knew it was going to nag at me. I don't like to intrude on my clients' privacy, but I nodded to Luke and told him, "Yeah, go ahead."

If the door was unlocked, we could call out again to Walter before we went in.

When Luke took hold of the knob and tried to turn it, though, it didn't move. He looked at me and shook his head. "Locked."

I thought about hunting up Tom Bradenton or one of the members of the resort staff to see if they could unlock the door. That seemed pretty extreme considering that it had only been about three hours since anybody had seen Walter, and he hadn't had firm plans to go back to Old Town with Ronnie no matter what she had assumed. He could already be there, in fact, partying hearty, although it was sort of hard to imagine Walter doing that.

"All right," I said. "We'll split up and look around for him. We've all got each other's cell phone numbers, so if one of us finds him, call the other two."

The sun was just setting, which meant the usual festivities were getting underway in Mallory Square. Street performers of all sorts flocked there, along with an abundance of food carts catering to the tourists watching the assorted shows. Walter might be right in the middle of the excitement, although, again, he didn't really seem the type.

I didn't expect Walter to be at any of the guest cottages scattered among the palm trees around the main house, since he wasn't exactly friends with any of the people staying in them, but I suggested that Ronnie walk around among them anyway.

"I'll take the stable and the pool," Luke said. I nodded in agreement. That left the tennis courts and the beach for me.

We split up and set off on our various paths. I followed a crushed coral walk toward the tennis courts, which were lit up so guests could play in the evening. As I approached I heard the regular *whack-whack-whack* rhythm of tennis balls being hit back and forth. I enjoyed tennis, but it had been a while since I played and I didn't figure I'd have time to get in a game while we were here.

The path curved around some shrubbery, and then I could see the two courts. They were well-lit, so I got a good look at the players and the other guests who were sitting on benches to the side with their rackets, waiting for a turn at the courts. Walter wasn't among them, just as I'd expected.

The path led past the courts, through some palm trees, and then out to the edge of the beach. As I stopped where the crushed coral ended, the southwestern sky seemed to open up around me, and without meaning to, I said, "Oh, my goodness."

The sun had already set, but not for long. The sky was still splashed with wide swathes of red and gold and pink and pale blue. It was beautiful enough to take my breath away. The broad sweep of ocean below that colorful vista of the heavens just made the view even more spectacular. A warm breeze caressed my face as I stood there for a minute just taking it all in.

With a little shake of my head, as if I were breaking the spell that Key West had cast on me, I reminded myself that I was here to look for Walter Harvick, not to gawk at the sunset. I lowered my eyes from the brilliant display and studied the people still on the beach. There were maybe two dozen of them, some playing volleyball, others splashing in the water, and others lying on towels or folding lounge chairs. The only ones I recognized were Matt and Aimee Altman, who were playing in the co-ed volleyball game. Aimee was wearing a white bikini so tiny it almost wasn't there.

No Walter.

Something else caught my eye, though. A catamaran was sailing through the water fairly close to the beach. Its sail had alternating stripes of brilliant red, blue, and yellow. The man at the tiller, if that's what the steering thing is called on a catamaran, seemed familiar, and he was close enough that I was able to recognize him as Tom

Bradenton. He wore only a brief bathing suit, and for a second I found myself thinking that he was just about as spectacular as that sunset.

Then the catamaran swept on past and the light continued to fade, and I knew I had failed in my mission to find Walter. I didn't feel any real sense of urgency about that. I still thought the most likely explanation for his disappearance was that he'd gone out on the town without Ronnie Scanlon. I wasn't going to let myself seriously consider any more sinister theory than that.

I went back to the main house, where I found Ronnie waiting for me on the verandah. I could tell by the anxious look on her face that she hadn't found Walter, either, and was hoping that I had. But when she saw that I was alone, she sighed.

"No luck?" she said.

I shook my head. "Afraid not. Maybe Luke spotted him."

A couple of minutes later Luke walked up, and he was by himself, too. When he reported that Walter was nowhere around the stable or the swimming pool, Ronnie still looked worried, but she was starting to look a little angry, too.

"He went off without me," she said. "That's the only explanation that makes any sense."

"Why don't you just go on to Old Town?" Luke suggested. "Maybe you'll run into him down there."

"No, if he doesn't want to spend time with me, I'm not going to force myself on him. It's just that I thought we were getting along better now."

I've never led a tour yet that didn't have a certain amount of soap opera involved in it. I said, "I'm going to Sloppy Joe's this evening. If I see him there, I'll read him the riot act."

Ronnie shook her head and said, "No, no, I

don't want you to do that, Ms. Dickinson. It's not really your problem."

That was true enough, but I actually did feel a little sympathetic toward her. I had dealt with my share of easily distracted and downright thoughtless men.

"I brought a couple of Hemingway books with me," Ronnie went on. "I think I'll go upstairs and just . . . just read."

She walked off. Luke watched her go and said quietly to me, "I'm sure glad I'm not single anymore. Too much drama." Probably remembering my marital status, he added quickly, "Not that there's anything wrong with – "

I stopped him by saying, "Don't worry about it. I'm not a big fan of all that drama, either."

Which was a little hypocritical considering some of the thoughts that had been going through my head about Tom, but I wasn't just about to get into that with Luke.

He said, "You really think Mr. Harvick is down on Duval Street?"

"He could be. I don't really know."

"You don't think that he . . . that maybe somebody . . ."

I fixed him with a firm stare. "Don't say it," I warned him. "Don't even think it."

"Sure, Miz D. It's just that it's been a while, and – "

"No, there you go again. Everything's fine, Luke. Take my word for it."

"Okay. You said you were going to Sloppy Joe's. You want me to run you over there in the van and drop you off?"

"No, I'll just take the resort shuttle. You don't mind stayin' here in case anybody needs anything this evening?"

"Not at all. Actually, George and Frank said something about getting together with Phil Thompson for a poker game. They invited me to sit in."

"Don't let 'em take your shirt."

"Hey, I'm a good poker player!" he protested. "Maybe Matt Altman would want to join us."

I thought about how Aimee had looked jumping around in that itty-bitty bikini while they were playing volleyball and said, "I doubt it."

Chapter 8

The resort's shuttle van dropped me off at the corner of Duval and Greene Streets, right in front of Sloppy Joe's. The sidewalks were crowded, despite the fairly early hour, and music pounded inside the bar and spilled out through the open doors. I was a little leery of going in there again, but actually nothing that terrible had happened the night before. Even the confrontation between Walter and Rollie hadn't really amounted to much.

I went inside, showing my ID to the gatekeeper at the door.

I was wearing capris, a lightweight blouse, and sandals. My hair looked about as good as anybody could reasonably expect in this humidity. I kept my little purse tight against my side and made my way through the throng toward the bar.

On the way there I happened to see one of the bouncers who'd been involved in the previous night's altercation. In fact, I almost literally ran into his broad, t-shirted chest. He moved aside, saying, "Sorry, ma'am," obviously with no memory of me. That wasn't surprising, considering how many people went through here every day and night.

He knew Rollie, though, I recalled, and had referred to him as one of the bar's regulars. So I raised my voice above the rock music and asked him, "Do you know if Rollie Cranston is here tonight?"

A grin stretched across his face. "You're one of Rollie's tourist ladies?"

It sounded like Rollie had a habit of making dates with female tourists who showed up at the Hemingway House. I would bet he was pretty successful at it, too, given his rugged good looks and – I agreed with Walter on this, to be honest – slight resemblance to Ernest Hemingway.

"Can you just tell me where he is?" I said to the bouncer.

"Sure." He pointed to a corner. Through narrow gaps in the crowd, I spotted a table there, under a big fake palm tree. Or maybe it was a real palm tree, I wasn't sure. But Rollie was sitting there, wearing a different shirt with bright tropical flowers on it.

"Thanks," I told the bouncer, then started weaving a path across the room.

Rollie had some sort of bright green drink in front of him. He saw me coming and stood up. He was a gentleman, anyway. A grin wreathed his whiskery face.

"Ms. Dickinson!" he greeted me. "I didn't know if you'd show up or not. Welcome! I'm glad you're here."

"You might as well call me Delilah," I said as I sat down on the other side of the small table.

He resumed his seat and said, "That's a beautiful name. It suits you. You won't cut off my beard, will you? I wouldn't look like Papa without it."

He didn't look that much like Papa with it, I thought, but I said, "Delilah in the Bible cut off Samson's hair. The Good Book doesn't say anything about her givin' him a shave."

"I'll bet you've heard plenty of jokes like that, though, haven't you?"

"More than my share," I admitted.

"What'll you drink?" He pointed to the glass in front of him. "This is one of the specialties of the house. Pretty potent, though. Think you can handle it?"

Some of the women Rollie cultivated probably felt like they had to accept that implied challenge. I wasn't one of them. I planned to keep a clear head tonight. I said, "I think a light beer will be fine."

He signaled to a young woman in shorts and a t-shirt who came over. He told her to bring me a light beer, and off she went to fetch it.

He leaned forward, resting his bare, brawny, deeply tanned forearms on the table, and asked, "Any more problems with that pipsqueak?"

"You're talkin' about one of my clients," I reminded him.

"Yeah, but that doesn't make him any less of a pipsqueak."

"He's been behaving himself."

"I'm glad to hear it." He toyed with the stem of his glass. "Sorry I lost my temper with him this afternoon. By now I ought to know to let all that guff roll off my back. All the buffs are full of it." He grinned again. "Buff guff. I think I've invented a new term."

Despite my wariness, I was warming up to him a little. He still wasn't my type and I didn't have any romantic interest in him, but he wasn't unlikeable.

The girl brought my beer in a sweat-dripping bottle. Rollie paid her for it, over my objections.

"I thought I was supposed to buy you a drink," I said when she was gone. "Wasn't that the deal?"

"The pleasure of your company is more than enough repayment for the trouble caused by that client of yours," he said. Then something across the room seemed to catch his attention. He turned his head a little, his eyes narrowed, and he muttered something I couldn't catch with the music blaring the way it was.

I leaned forward and asked, "What was that?"

"I said, speak of the devil. He's here."

"Who?"

"Your client. The pipsqueak."

I looked across the room where Rollie was looking, and sure enough, Walter Harvick was standing there at the bar, talking to a man I'd never seen before. I could only see part of the stranger's face because of the way he was turned. He had a shock of very dark hair, a tanned, weathered face, and an equally dark mustache under a nose like a hawk's beak.

"What's he doing with Clint Drake?" Rollie asked.

"Clint Drake?" I repeated. "That's the other guy's name?"

"Don't let the movie star name fool you," Rollie said. "Or the fact that he looks like Gilbert Roland."

I figured there weren't very many people in Sloppy Joe's tonight who would recognize the name Gilbert Roland. I was one of 'em, though, and I saw that Rollie was right. Clint Drake bore a distinct resemblance to the old movie actor.

"He's kind of a bad guy," Rollie went on. "Owns a charter boat and works as a fishing guide, but the rumor is that he's not too particular about the charters he takes out. If you've got the money to pay his price, Drake's your guy, no matter what you're up to."

"Are you sayin' he smuggles drugs?" I asked.

Rollie shrugged. "Drugs, guns, illegal aliens. Drake doesn't care as long as you can pay."

In a place as bright and beautiful as Key West, you'd like to think that crime doesn't even exist. Unfortunately, that isn't true. No matter where you go, there's always somebody willing to break the law if it gets them what they want. In the travel business we warn our clients of any dangers we know about, and we try to keep an eye on them as much as we can, but there's only so much we can do.

If Rollie was telling the truth – and the only reason I could think of for him to be lying to me was to make himself seem more dashing because he knew something about a shady character – then this was one of those situations where I needed to steer a client away from potential trouble.

I got to my feet. Rollie said, "Wait a minute. Where are you going? You just got here."

"If that fella Drake's as bad as you say he is, I need to get Walter away from him."

"Walter's a grown man," Rollie objected. "As much as he ever will be, anyway."

"My job is to look after my clients. That includes tryin' to keep them from getting into trouble in the first place."

Rollie muttered something again, then put his hands on the table and shoved himself to his feet.

"If you're determined to stick your nose in, I'd better go with you."

I felt a flash of anger at that comment. I didn't

like being accused of sticking my nose in where it didn't belong. But at the same time I was grateful to him for volunteering to come along, although I knew there was also a chance Rollie's presence would just upset Walter.

I led the way, weaving through the crowd that eddied back and forth. Because of the constant press of people around me, sometimes I couldn't see the bar. After one of those moments, when the spot where Walter and Drake had been standing came back into view, the two of them were gone. My breath caught in my throat. What if Walter had left Sloppy Joe's with Drake? Was he in danger?

Then I spotted them again. They weren't gone yet, but they were heading for the doors.

"Walter!" I called. "Walter! Hey!"

He didn't look back. I couldn't tell if he didn't hear me because of the music and the noisy crowd, or if he was just ignoring me. But I started pushing through the throng in a more urgent manner, drawing a few complaints along the way that I ignored. I hoped Rollie was still behind me, but I didn't look back to be sure.

I caught up to them on the sidewalk right outside the door. "Walter!" I said again, and even though the music was still loud out here, I knew he had to be able to hear me.

He paused and turned halfway around. "Ms. Dickinson," he said. "What can I do for you?"

"We've been lookin' for you, Walter," I said. "Why didn't you answer your cell phone?" I kept my attention on him and tried not to look at Drake, but even from the corner of my eye I could see the scowl on the man's face. He didn't like being interrupted.

"I guess I didn't hear it with all the racket in

there," Walter said. "And you said we. Who's we? Ronnie's not with you, is she?"

"No, she's back at the resort. But she's worried about you, Walter. She thought the two of you were going out together tonight."

"I didn't make any firm commitment to that. She mentioned it, but I didn't promise anything."

Yep, ass hat, I thought. But I said, "I know she'd really like to see you. A shuttle bus ought to be along any minute. Why don't we catch it and go back?"

He frowned and shook his head. "I can't. I'm busy – "

He was interrupted by Rollie, who shouldered up beside me and said, "Hello, Drake."

"Cranston," Drake said curtly.

The crazy thought that it was like a scene from a movie struck me as the two of them faced each other. I felt like the camera should zoom in on each of them in turn as they squinted at each other, while Spaghetti Western music welled up in the background.

Then Walter broke the tense mood by saying to Rollie, "You! What are you doing here?"

"Trying to keep you from making a mistake, ace," Rollie said.

Walter sneered and said, "I don't need any advice from a bumpkin who knows less about Ernest Hemingway than my pet goldfish does."

"Now, Walter," I said, moving between them, "there's no need to talk like that. Rollie's just tryin' to help – "

"So the two of you are friends now," Walter broke in. He shook his head. "I must say, I'm a little disappointed in you, Ms. Dickinson."

He sure made it hard to give a flying fig what happened to him. I just reminded myself that he was a client, though, and pressed on.

"Come on back inside and have a drink with us," I urged.

"With him?" Walter looked at Rollie and shook his head again, this time in complete, unmistakable contempt. "I don't think so."

"You should go ahead with them, sport," Clint Drake said. "I've already told you, I can't help you, and trailing after me isn't going to make a bit of difference."

That surprised me a little. I had thought that Walter and Drake were leaving Sloppy Joe's together, but now that I thought about it, I decided it was possible Walter had been following the shady charter boat captain, trying to talk him into some-thing.

Walter must not have had enough money to hire Drake, I thought. According to Rollie, that was the only thing that would have made any difference to Drake.

Walter turned to Drake and said quickly, "But Captain – "

"Better listen to him," Rollie said. "Steering clear of him is the smartest thing you'll ever do."

"You should take your own advice, Cranston," Drake said. He moved toward us a little, squaring his shoulders.

I figured there was about to be a fistfight, but at that moment, someone called out, "Walter!"

It was Ronnie Scanlon, of course. She had just stepped down from the shuttle bus that had pulled up at the curb without me noticing. She hurried across the crowded sidewalk, bobbing and weaving around pedestrians, and threw her arms around Walter as she came up to him.

He didn't try to get away from her as she planted a big kiss on his lips.

Chapter 9

That kiss packed enough passion in it to keep Walter rooted to the spot as the seconds ticked by. When Ronnie finally pulled back, both of them were a little wide-eyed and breathless.

The effect didn't last long. Walter looked around and exclaimed, "He's gone!"

I didn't have to ask who he was talking about. It was true. While Rollie and I were watching Ronnie plant that big smacker on Walter, Clint Drake had vanished into the crowds along Duval Street.

Walter jerked his head frantically from side to side as he searched for some sign of Drake, but after a moment he had to give up. He turned toward Ronnie again and went on, "What have you done?"

Rollie drawled, "I'd say the lady has done you a big favor. I'm talking about her being willing to kiss you, of course, but in addition to that, she saved you from possibly winding up in jail . . . or worse."

"What are you talking about?" Walter demanded.

"Clint Drake. He's a criminal."

"Nonsense. He was highly recommended to me as a charter boat captain who knows the Keys better than anyone else. That's just the sort of man I need."

"Whoever told you that was probably one of Drake's crooked cronies," Rollie said. "You're better off staying as far away from the likes of him as possible."

It crossed my mind to wonder what Walter needed with a charter boat captain, but that didn't really seem important just then. I said, "Now that Ronnie's here, let's all go inside and have a drink."

I figured Walter would argue, but he sighed and said, "We might as well." He nodded toward Rollie and added, "Not with him, though."

"You're not my idea of pleasant company, either," Rollie said. "And the lady's with me."

He put his arm around my shoulders.

I didn't want to offend Rollie, but I moved out of that embrace as discreetly as I could. It wasn't discreet enough to keep a look of hurt from briefly crossing his face.

"Oh," he said. "Well, I suppose the time we spent together will have to do, Delilah. It was pleasant . . . up to a point. I suppose I was presumptuous, wasn't I?"

"Just a little," I told him. "I'm not holdin' any grudges if you aren't."

He waved a hand and grinned. "Nah. Nothing was ever going to come of it anyway, was it?"

"I'm afraid not. I'll be leavin' in a couple of days."

"Of course. Let me give you a hug."

I didn't object to that. It was actually a pretty nice hug. When it was over he lifted a hand in a little salute and turned to go back into Sloppy

Joe's.

I didn't think it would be a very good idea for Walter and Ronnie to be drinking in there, so I turned to them and suggested, "Why don't we go around the corner to Captain Tony's?"

At first I didn't think Walter was going to go for it, but he said, "I suppose that's all right. I wanted to go there while I was in Key West anyway. It was the location of the original Sloppy Joe's, you know. Joe Russell, the owner of the bar, got in an argument with the landlord over the rent and moved around here to this location in 1937. Hemingway actually spent a lot more time in what's now Captain Tony's than he did in here."

I already knew that, but I didn't burst Walter's bubble by pointing it out. Instead, I motioned for Ronnie to take one of his arms and I took the other, and the three of us started off, turning at the corner to go along Greene Street.

This was probably the first time in his life Walter Harvick had a good-looking woman on each arm, I thought, then told myself it was sort of immodest of me to be thinking that, not to mention a little mean. But true anyway.

I leaned past him to say to Ronnie, "I thought you were going to spend the evening at the resort."

"Well, I was planning to," she said. "But I got so worried about Walter here."

"You were worried about me, really?" he said. "There was no need to be. I know exactly what I'm doing."

Unfortunately, just because somebody knew what they were doing didn't mean there was no reason to worry about them.

We followed a brick sidewalk along Greene. Ahead of us, a big stuffed fish hung out over the sidewalk, above a sign that proclaimed *CAPT. TONY'S SALOON The First and Original Sloppy Joe's 1933 – 1937.* Not surprisingly, there was also a picture of Ernest Hemingway on the sign.

Now that Walter was away from Sloppy Joe's and away from both Rollie Cranston and Clint Drake as well, I was sort of a third wheel. As we stopped at the door of Captain Tony's, I said, "Why don't the two of you go on inside and enjoy yourselves? I really ought to be gettin' back to the resort."

"I thought you were going to have a drink with us," Walter said.

"Yeah, but you have each other. You don't need me around."

Walter raised an eyebrow and said, "We're hardly alone." He gestured toward the hundreds of people along the sidewalks.

"Two people can be alone together no matter how many others are all around them," I said. I thought that was pretty romantic, and Ronnie seemed to like it.

"Come on, Walter," she said. "I really want to spend more time with you."

"I suppose that would be all right." He looked at me like he had suddenly realized something. "You're going back to Sloppy Joe's to find that . . . that imposter, aren't you?"

"No, Walter, I'm not," I told him honestly. "I'm tired, and I'm going back to the resort to go to bed."

Alone, I added to myself.

Which, for some doggone reason, made me think about Tom Bradenton, a thought that I banished from my mind as quickly as I could.

Maybe not quite quickly enough.

For Whom The Funeral Bell Tolls

* * *

While I waited for the next resort shuttle to come along, I watched the tide of people flowing in and out of Sloppy Joe's. They were all ages, shapes, and sizes, and as usual, there was nothing more fascinating than people. I had told Walter the truth, though. I really was tired. So I was glad to climb on board the shuttle and make the ride back across the island to the resort.

It was plenty early enough this evening so that nobody would have to let me in. I told myself I wasn't disappointed by that. But I'd be lying if I said my heart didn't jump a little when I saw Tom Bradenton walking across the grounds toward the main house, moving in and out of patches of light and shadow caused by the electric lights in the trees.

I slowed down a little so we'd reach the verandah about the same time. He smiled at me and said, "Hello. Been out partying in Old Town?"

He was wearing jeans, canvas shoes, and a faded blue work shirt with the sleeves rolled up a couple of turns. A rag in his hand was smeared with the reddish-black sheen of engine grease. I pointed toward it and said, "You're the one who looks like you've been partyin'."

He held up the rag and laughed. "Yeah, if you count wrestling with a balky old carburetor as a party. I've been working on my boat."

"I saw you sailing on a catamaran earlier, just at sunset," I said. I didn't mention how impressed I'd been by the sight. "I didn't know you had a boat with an engine, too."

"Yeah, an old fishing boat. It belonged to my great-grandfather, actually. I like to go out and putter around the Gulf in it sometimes. The engine's got a problem right now, though, and I can't seem to get it licked." He folded the rag so the grease was on the inside of it and stuck it in the hip pocket of his jeans. "Forget about that old scow. It's slow, anyway. If you're interested, I'd be glad to take you out on the cat."

Now that was an appealing idea, I thought. I'd never sailed on a catamaran before. I could just imagine gliding fast and smooth over the water with Tom beside me . . .

Then I remembered that I didn't like the water, didn't swim particularly well, and got seasick really easily. I wasn't sure how much a catamaran bounced around, but as lightweight as they were, I figured that sailing on one might be a pretty wild ride.

I gave Tom a regretful smile and said, "Sorry, I'm not much of a sailor."

"Well, I'm sure we could find something else to do."

I wasn't sure if he was flirting or just being friendly. I voted for flirting, so I said, "I'd like that."

"Right now, for instance, a walk on the beach might be nice," he suggested.

I decided I wasn't that tired after all. "Sure," I said.

We fell in step together on the coral path that curved through the trees toward the beach. As we walked I asked, "Where do you keep your boats? I haven't seen them while we've been here."

"There's a little dock off at the side of the property, beyond the stable," he said, gesturing vaguely in that direction. "They're both tied up there. I try to do a little sailing two or three times a week. I like to be out on the water by myself. Seems like that's the only place quiet and peaceful enough for my brain to really relax." He paused. "Not that I mind having company sometimes. That's always good, too."

"I'll bet it is," I said. I wondered how many women he had taken out on that catamaran.

Probably almost as many as he'd wanted to, I was willing to bet. The ones who turned down his invitation were likely few and far between.

"I used to take fishing charters out," he went on, "but that got to be too much work." Even in the shadows under the trees I saw the flash of his teeth as he grinned. "What's the point of owning a place like this if you can't be lazy when you want to?"

"I run my own business, too," I reminded him. "I know how much work goes into it. It's not a job for somebody who's lazy."

"No, that's true," he admitted. "It's been a challenge keeping this place up and running. I don't have billions of dollars of corporate money behind me like the chains do. But there are more than enough perks to make it worth doing."

"Same here," I said. And one of those perks, I added to myself, was meeting interesting people like him.

We reached the beach. At this hour it was deserted. The folks who had still been there right after sunset had drifted on back to the main house or to their cabins as night settled in.

The moon was high enough to scatter silvery light, and the white sand reflected the glow so that while it wasn't as bright as day out here, we had no trouble seeing as we walked along. Tom and I both took off our shoes to make walking in the sand easier. I had my sandals in my right hand, his shoes were in his left. That made it easy for him to reach over with his right hand and clasp my left. There was nothing awkward about it. It felt as natural as can be.

"This is beautiful," I murmured. The waves whispered in on our left, and stars twinkled in the black sky overhead. Key West gave off enough light pollution to wash out some of them, but I could still see a lot more stars here than were ever visible back home in Atlanta. "There are so many of them."

Tom seemed to know what I was talking about. He said, "You should see them sometime when you're out on the ocean or the Gulf, far away from anything. The whole sky is covered with little pinpoints of light. It's amazing."

"I'm sure it is."

He came to a stop, and we turned toward each other. He said, "Amazing," again and leaned toward me.

His shoes hit the ground, and my sandals joined them a second later. Our arms went around each other.

A handsome man, a beach, moonlight, a million stars . . . It would have been going against fate if I *didn't* kiss him.

So I did, and it was every bit as good as I expected it to be.

But no matter how good it was – and my heart was pounding when we broke that kiss, let me tell you – I knew I was barreling right toward a mistake. Two more days and I'd be headed home, and I just wasn't the type for a one night stand. Or even a two night stand, for that matter. After that I might not ever see Tom Brandenton again.

Until the next time I brought a tour group to Key West, I reminded myself.

Still, I didn't much believe in long-distance

relationships, either. There were just too many things working against it, no matter how good it felt to have Tom's arms around me and the taste of his lips lingering on mine.

"I . . . need to go back in," I whispered. "To my room. Alone."

"Are you sure about that?" he asked me.

Good grief, no, I wasn't sure! That's what I wanted to yell. But the rational, reasonable part of my brain made me say, "Yeah, I'm sure."

"Okay." He rested his hands on my shoulders. "We had a nice walk on the beach, anyway, didn't we?"

"Really nice," I said.

"And you're not leaving for a couple of days yet. Maybe we can do this again."

"Maybe," I said, although I thought it would probably be a mistake on my part if we did. I might not be able to be this strong again.

"Can I walk you back to the main house?" he asked.

"You'd better," I told him. I bent and picked up my sandals, he got his shoes, and we turned back toward the trees and the path to the house.

He took my hand again. I didn't pull away.

The next two days, I thought, were going to be mighty interesting.

Chapter 10

I made it back to my room without my resolve weakening enough to make me give in to what I really wanted to do. I even went to sleep without too much tossing and turning first, although I was a little restless.

Sometime during the night something woke me. I rolled over, blinked bleary-eyed, and sat up to look toward the window. I even got out of bed and walked over to the window to move the shade aside and look out. Nothing but darkness relieved here and there by the lights in the trees, which had been turned down so that they were only dim glows. I listened and heard only the faint hum of the air-conditioning. Not having any idea what had disturbed my sleep, I went back to bed and crawled under the sheet.

I didn't even glance at the clock, which was on the other side of the bed from the window.

I dozed off again without much trouble, and nothing else bothered me until somebody started pounding on my door like he was trying to knock it down. When I jerked upright in the bed, I glanced toward the window and saw light coming around the shade. It was morning.

And something was wrong. I could tell that from the urgency of whoever was hammering at my door.

I stood up, grabbed my robe, and shrugged into it. I dragged my fingers through my hair, trying to get some of the sleep tangles out of it, as I stumbled toward the door. When I got there, I called, "Who is it?" As soon as the words were out of my mouth, I realized I could have looked through the little peephole to see who was being so heavy-handed.

The reply came back before I could do that. "It's Luke, Miz D. We've got trouble."

"Oh, Lord," I muttered. No tour ever goes off without a single hitch, but for some reason I'd sort of been holding my breath ever since we'd gotten to Key West, hoping that nothing too bad would happen. From the sound of Luke's voice, that hope had been futile.

I unfastened the deadbolt and pulled the door open. He stood there with his hair tangled from sleep, too. He had dressed in a hurry, pulling on a t-shirt and a pair of jeans and sticking his feet in sandals.

"What is it?" I asked him. "Tell me somebody's not dead. Please."

"I don't know about dead, but somebody's bound to be hurt. The cops are here, and an ambulance, and that guy Tom Bradenton told me to find you. I ran into him in the lobby when I went down to see what was going on. The sirens woke me up."

I had slept right through them.

"Tom didn't tell you what was going on?" I asked.

Luke shook his head. "No, just that I should find you and bring you down to the beach."

If I'd been the type to cuss, I'd have let loose with a few blue howlers just then. I didn't know what had happened, but I was sure it was bad enough. The fact that it had happened on the beach where I had gone walking with Tom . . . where we had kissed . . . just made it that much worse.

"Hang on," I told Luke. "I'll be ready in a minute."

I shut the door. The clothes I'd been wearing the night before were still handy, lying on a chair. I got into them as fast as I could, grabbed my phone from the bedside table, and stuck it in my pocket as I was stepping into my sandals. Then I opened the door and said to Luke, "Let's go."

I didn't hear any commotion as we went downstairs, so I supposed all the sirens had gone silent. Nobody else was moving around the main house, either, which told me the hour was early. We passed a clock in the lobby. A glance told me it was a few minutes after six o'clock in the morning. The sun was up, but just barely.

Luke groaned as we went outside. "Does it have to be so bright already?" he said.

"Let me guess. You did some drinkin' along with your poker playin' last night?"

"I didn't think I drank that much. I guess I'm not really used to rum."

"Yo ho ho and a bottle of," I said.

"Don't joke about it, Miz D," he pleaded. "That sunlight's like knives in my eyes."

"You'll get used to it," I told him.

I didn't explain that I was joking only to take my mind off what we were about to find out. I knew it couldn't be anything good, and I had a hunch it was going to be pretty bad.

Several police cars and an ambulance, all with their lights flashing, were parked in the lot to the side of the main house, but I didn't see anybody around them. I heard the crackle of radio chatter coming from the vehicles. Luke and I kept moving.

Tom Bradenton came around a bend in the path ahead of us. He looked shaken and upset, and when he spotted us his face grew even more haggard. He held up a hand and said, "Delilah, I think you'd better stop right there."

"You sent Luke to find me and bring me to the beach," I reminded him.

"Yeah, but now I think you don't need to see this," he told me with a shake of his head.

That made me angry. If the problem was something that involved me or one of my clients, then I didn't want anybody trying to keep me out of it. It wasn't like this was my first rodeo, either. I had been knee-deep in trouble several times in the past.

"No offense, Tom, but get out of my way," I said. "I need to know what's going on, so I can deal with it."

Tom shook his head again and said, "There's no dealing with this."

Dreading what I was going to see, I moved past him and walked quickly toward the beach. My stride was firm and determined, but it was definitely at odds with what was going on inside me. A big part of me wanted to turn around and run the other way as fast as I could. The responsible part wouldn't let me do that . . . damn it.

The trees opened up on the broad stretch of white sand that ran as far in both directions as the eye could see. Against that pristine beauty, the thing that lay on the sand about halfway from where I stood to the water was shockingly ugly and out of place. It was a man's body, lying on its back. That would have been bad enough by itself.

The fact that the body didn't have a head, or a whole head, anyway, made it even worse. Much worse.

I stopped in my tracks and swallowed hard. I wasn't the queasy type, but if I had eaten recently, I think I would have lost it then.

As it was, Luke came up beside me, stopped just as abruptly as I had, and gulped a couple of times before he turned and dashed off into the trees.

My heart pounded so hard it felt like it might burst right out of my chest. I willed myself to stay calm and glanced around as I heard a foostep. Tom came up behind me. I thought the clothes on the body looked familiar, but I said, "Do . . . do you know who it is?"

"It's Mr. Harvick," he said. "That's what I heard one of the cops say when he checked the ID in the poor guy's wallet."

"Walter," I whispered.

Several men were standing around the body, not getting too close, all of them in police uniforms except for one. He hunkered closer to Walter, obviously studying the scene intently. The ambulance crew stood off to the side, waiting with a gurney and a body bag.

Something else caught my attention. I said, "What's that lying on the sand beside him? Is it . . ."

"A shotgun," Tom said. "That's right. From the looks of it, he, uh, put the barrels in his mouth and used his toe to, uh . . ."

He shook his head, so horrified that he was unable to finish.

"Just like Hemingway," I said, and even I could hear how hollow my voice sounded.

"His idol, I guess."

I turned to look at Tom. "But that happened in Idaho, not Key West."

"I know. It doesn't make sense to me, either."

I forced my brain to start working again and asked, "Who found him?"

"Those two elderly ladies in your group. Mrs. Horton and Mrs. Dunn. They said they got up early to come down here and walk on the beach before it got crowded."

The beach wouldn't be crowded today, I thought, except with cops. It was a crime scene now.

Then I spared a moment to think about how terrible that must have been for Doris and Julia. They must have been shocked beyond belief to find Walter like that. I would have to talk to them as soon as possible and offer what little comfort I could.

"Do you have any idea when it happened?"

"The ladies came down here about thirty minutes before sun-up," Tom said. "Sometime before that is all I know."

I thought about being woken up in the middle of the night. Something had disturbed me, and a shotgun blast is pretty loud. Could I have heard it all the way from the beach, even with the window in my room closed? It was possible, I thought. Under the circumstances, maybe even likely.

I wished I had thought to look at the clock while I was up. Telling the cops that I woke up during the night wouldn't mean anything. Telling them that I woke up at a specific hour might have been helpful if they were able to establish an approximate time of death for Walter.

Luke joined us at the edge of the beach. His step was none too steady and he still looked a little green. "Man," he said, "I've never seen anything like that before . . . and I never want to see anything like it again!" He had to swallow. "Is that Mr. Harvick?"

"Yeah," I said. "Poor Walter."

"Why would anybody do something like that to themselves? I just don't get it."

Neither did I. In all the time I'd spent with him, Walter hadn't once struck me as suicidal. Arrogant, opinionated, downright unpleasant at times, sure, but not suicidal.

The man who had been studying the body stood up and came toward us. Like so many men in Key West, he wore a lightweight shirt with bright flowers on it, along with khaki trousers and tennis shoes. He was black, probably a couple of inches over six feet, with a broad spread of shoulders and a pleasantly ugly face. As he came up to us, he reached in his pocket and took out a leather folder that he opened to reveal a badge.

"Detective Zimmer, Key West PD," he introduced himself. "Are you Ms. Dickinson?"

"That's right," I told him. In khakis and flowery shirt, he didn't look much like a cop, but that was Key West for you.

"Good," he said in his deep, powerful voice. "I've got some questions for you."

Chapter 11

"His name was Walter Harvick," I said, "and the credit card number he gave me was good. That's really all I know about him, Detective."

"Surely you know more than that, Ms. Dickinson," Zimmer said. "You spent a day and a half with the man, isn't that right?"

"Only part of the time. I met him in Miami day before yesterday, when my tour group assembled to come down here, but we haven't been together all the time since then."

We were still standing at the edge of the beach, but I had turned so that I didn't have to look in the direction where Walter's body was. Zimmer didn't seem to mind. He had asked Luke and Tom to go back to the house and wait for him there. I wasn't sure why he didn't conduct his interview with me at the house, too, unless he was suspicious of me for some reason and wanted me close to the body in the hope that it would make me uncomfortable.

It certainly did, make me uncomfortable, that is, even though Zimmer had no reason to be suspicious of me. I guess he didn't know that, though.

"How did Mr. Harvick behave during the trip?" Zimmer asked now. "Did he get along with all the other tourists?"

I hesitated. I know I shouldn't have, but I couldn't help myself. And I could tell by the flicker of interest in Zimmer's eyes that he noticed, too.

"Mr. Harvick didn't really have that much to do with the other tourists," I said. "I guess he got along all right with them."

"Except the ones he had problems with," Zimmer said. "Or was there only one?"

"There weren't really any problems. Just minor disagreements. Irritations. You know, the kind of things that happen when people who don't really know each other have to spend time together."

"Tell me about them," Zimmer urged.

I could see that he wasn't going to be satisfied until I told him what he wanted to know, so I said, "Mr. Harvick got into a little argument with one of my other clients at the Hemingway House yesterday. But it didn't amount to anything. There were hardly any harsh words exchanged."

Zimmer took a small notebook and a pen from his shirt pocket. The detective's best friends. "What was this person's name? The one Harvick had the argument with?"

"Matt Altman. He's here with his wife Aimee. They're not much more than kids. Haven't been married long."

"Honeymooners, eh?" Zimmer wrote in the notebook and shook his head. "You'd think they'd have better things to do than squabble with another tourist."

"Yeah, you'd think so," I agreed. "But like I said, it didn't really amount to much."

"Who else had trouble with Harvick?"

"I wouldn't really call it trouble. He had a little romance going on with one of the other tour members."

"Male or female?"

"Female," I said. "As far as I could tell, Mr. Harvick was straight."

"Uh-huh. What's the woman's name?"

"Veronica Scanlon. She goes by Ronnie," I added, although I didn't see how knowing that would do Zimmer any good.

"Lots of arguments between them? Hurt feelings?"

"Not really. It's just that I don't think Walter took their relationship quite as seriously as Ronnie did. You can't really blame him for that. They'd known each other less than twelve hours when it started."

Zimmer wrote in his notebook again. When he finished, I said, "Can I ask you something, Detective?"

"Go ahead."

"From the way you're talking, it sounds almost like you think Walter, Mr. Harvick, might have been murdered. I thought he, uh, committed suicide."

Zimmer's massive shoulders rose and fell an inch or so. "That's certainly what it looks like. The scene's consistent with that finding. But that's not up to me to determine. The medical examiner will be here soon. In the meantime, I thought I ought to find out as much as I could about the situation. And being a detective . . ." He surprised me with a big grin. "Homicide is sort of what first comes to mind, you know?"

I knew. It was the first thing I had thought, too,

when I saw the police cars and the ambulance. But that was the same sort of response that a body lying on a beach with its head more than half blown off would garner, no matter who pulled the trigger.

"Did Harvick seem suicidal to you?" Zimmer went on.

I had to shake my head and say, "No, not really. But I've never actually been around anybody who . . . who did that. So I don't know. I run a travel agency. I'm not a clinical psychologist."

"Neither am I. Who else had trouble with Harvick?"

The sudden shift in the conversation, back to interrogation mode, almost threw me. That was probably what Zimmer was counting on.

"As far as I know, he got along fine with everybody else on my tour," I said.

"What about people who weren't on your tour?"

I had hoped he wouldn't catch that angle. But he had, so I didn't see that I had any choice but to answer. If Zimmer backtracked the tour, he would find out about what had happened at the Hemingway House anyway.

"He got into an argument with one of the guides at the Hemingway House," I said. "As a matter of fact, Walter sort of got into it with the same fella the night before that at Sloppy Joe's. He was one of the Hemingway look-alikes, and he didn't much like it when Walter told him he didn't look anything like Hemingway."

"You know this man's name?"

"Rollie Cranston."

I hated throwing Rollie under the bus like that, but I figured that the medical examiner would say Walter had killed himself and any sort of murder investigation would be over before it really got started. I was hoping that Detective Zimmer would not even have to talk to Ronnie Scanlon or the Altmans or Rollie Cranston.

"I know Rollie," Zimmer said as he made a note of the name. "Seems like a pretty good guy."

"Yeah, I thought so, too."

Zimmer frowned slightly at me. "Even though he had trouble with one of your clients?"

"Just because they're my clients, Detective, doesn't mean they're automatically right about everything. Walter's attitude rubbed Rollie the wrong way. I can't say that I blame him for that."

"Okay. Anything else you need to tell me, Ms. Dickinson?"

I thought back for a moment and said, "Last night at Sloppy Joe's, Walter was talking to a man named Clint Drake."

That got Zimmer's interest, all right. "Drake," he repeated, obviously familiar with the name. "What in the world did the two of them have to do with each other?"

"You'd have to ask Mr. Drake," I said. "I got the impression that Walter tried to charter Mr. Drake's boat, but Mr. Drake didn't want the job."

"Why would Harvick try to charter a boat? Why didn't he arrange that through you?"

I could only shake my head and say, "I don't have any idea. I actually do have a boat chartered for tomorrow. Some of my clients are going out deep-sea fishing. Walter didn't seem to have any interest in going along on that trip."

"What boat?" Zimmer asked, but he just sounded curious this time, less like a police detective.

"The *Lightning Bolt*."

He nodded. "Eddie Garcia's boat. I know it."

I was starting to get the impression that he knew everybody on Key West, all the locals, anyway. Which wouldn't be that surprising. It's a small island, after all, and many of the Conch families have been there for a long time.

"How about the *Mary Lou*?" I asked out of curiosity to see if he knew that one.

"Sure. Jimmy Malone's the skipper? Why do you ask?"

"One of my clients chartered it yesterday to go fishing."

From the direction of the main house, an older, rawboned man came along the path toward us carrying a black bag. Zimmer half-turned and pointed.

"The body's out there, Doctor."

"Thanks," the doctor said. "I probably would have completely overlooked a bloody, headless body lying in the middle of the beach."

Zimmer smiled and shook his head a little as the man went on past us.

"The medical examiner?" I asked.

"That's right. His sarcasm is sharper than his scalpel." Zimmer turned his attention back to me. "What else can you tell me about Walter Harvick? Where's he from? Do you have any next-of-kin info for him?"

"There should be an emergency contact listed on the paperwork he filled out for my agency, and that'll have his home address on it, too. All that information is back at my office, but I can get it. My daughter runs the office, and all I'd have to do is call her or email her."

Zimmer took a card from his pocket and held it out to me. "Could you have her just email the form to me at that address?"

"I could," I said as I took the card from him,

"but there are privacy issues, Detective. Shouldn't you have a warrant or a court order for that sort of information?"

"Technically, I suppose so, but since you seemed willing to cooperate . . ."

"Oh, I am," I said quickly. "But I think I should talk to my lawyer before I turn over any information Mr. Harvick gave me."

That answer didn't seem to bother him. He said, "Fine, we probably won't need copies of all that paperwork anyway. We should contact his next of kin as soon as possible, though."

"I can get that for you," I said.

"Is there anything else you can tell me about Walter Harvick?"

I thought about it and shook my head. "Nope. That's it."

"But it was a lot more than what you claimed you could tell me at first, wasn't it?"

I didn't have to answer that because the medical examiner came back then. He said, "When can I have the body, Charles?"

"Any time, Doc," Zimmer replied. "We've already photographed the scene and searched it. Nothing to find, really, beyond the obvious."

"Yes, that's usually the case, isn't it, when a man blows his head off? There's no doubt about the cause of death, but I'll do a post-mortem anyway." The doctor shook his head and added in a tone of disgust, "Hemingway."

As he plodded off, I asked Zimmer, "What did he mean by that?"

"This isn't the first case of suicide by shotgun we've seen," Zimmer said. "It's not that common or anything, but every so often someone obsessed with Hemingway decides to come down here and kill himself."

"After all this time? That was more than fifty years ago, and it didn't even happen here."

"I know. Some people are nuts for certain writers, though, and Hemingway makes it easy. The fans can go to Spain and go to the bullfights or run with the bulls in Pamplona, or they can go to Africa and hunt big game, or they can go out on the ocean and try to hook a big fish. I guess when they've done all that . . . what else is left except putting the barrels of a shotgun in their mouth?"

I didn't have an answer for him. I was still trying not to be sick as I glanced at the beach and saw the ambulance crew zipping something ugly into that body bag.

Chapter 12

Detective Zimmer told me I could go back up to the main house. "You're not leaving town until the day after tomorrow, though, right?" he asked.

"That's right," I said.

He nodded. "Maybe we won't need you any more by then."

What he meant was that maybe by then they would have an official determination that Walter Harvick had committed suicide and there was no reason to conduct any further investigation. Tragic though it might be, that was the outcome I was hoping for.

As I walked through the palm trees, I took the phone from my pocket and thumbed the speed-dial for Melissa's phone. A moment later I heard my daughter's sleepy voice saying, "Mom? What's wrong?"

"How do you know something's wrong?" I asked her.

"Well, it's awfully early in the morning. Not quite seven o'clock yet."

"I'm sorry I woke you."

"No, no, that's fine," Melissa said. "What is it?"

"I need you to access the office computer, get an emergency contact number for one of our clients, and email it to my phone." She could do all that without leaving the apartment she shared with Luke.

"Oh, no," she said. "Somebody's had an accident, haven't they?"

"You could say that." But it wouldn't really be true, I thought. What had happened wasn't really an accident. "It looks like one of the members of the group has killed himself."

"No." Melissa's voice was hushed with horror. "Who would do such a thing?"

She hadn't met any of these clients, so the name wouldn't really mean anything to her, but she'd need it to get his emergency contact number. "Walter Harvick," I told her.

"I remember the name. I'll look up that information and get it to you right away, Mom. Are you all right?"

"I'm fine," I told her. Shaken up, no doubt about that, but I was holding it together, I thought.

"You're sure it was suicide? Mr. Harvick wasn't . . ."

She didn't say it, so I did. "Murdered? There's no indication of that, as far as I know."

"Well, that's good, anyway, no matter how terrible the rest of it is. I just thought . . ."

Again she couldn't finish her sentence. I said, "I know what you thought, honey. The same thing occurred to me. But I'm keepin' my fingers crossed that's not the way it turns out this time. We ought to know later today, or maybe tomorrow."

"All right. I'll send that information to you as soon as I can."

"Thanks," I told her.

"How's Luke?" she asked before I could break the connection.

The last time I'd seen him, he was hungover and green around the gills from chucking up at the sight of Walter's corpse. But I didn't see any point in telling Melissa about that, so I just said, "He's fine." He could always give her more of the details later on if he wanted to.

"All right. Let me know if you need anything else."

I told her I would, then said goodbye and ended the call. I had reached the main house. Luke and Tom were waiting on the verandah.

"Did Charles finish his interrogation?" Tom asked. "He must have, or you wouldn't be here."

"You and Detective Zimmer know each other?"

"Of course. Key West is actually a pretty small place," he added, echoing the same thought I'd had earlier.

"Yeah, he finished asking his questions, and the medical examiner came and took the body. I suppose he'll want to talk to the two of you. Detective Zimmer, I mean."

"I'll help him any way I can," Tom said, "but I don't know much of anything. Those two ladies who found the body came in really upset. There was already a clerk on duty at the desk, and she came to get me. I hurried down to the beach, had a quick look, and came back up here long enough to tell Luke to find you. Then I headed back down there in case the cops needed me."

"And I know even less," Luke said.

I said, "Well, if it turns out to be suicide the way it looks, it won't take long to close the case. Maybe we'll be able to salvage some of the rest of the tour . . . if anybody's still in the mood for it."

"What else could it be except suicide?" Tom asked. "When you stick a gun in your mouth and pull the trigger, that's pretty much a foregone conclusion."

"Yeah," I agreed. Given my history, I was still nervous about the whole deal, though.

I wondered if Detective Zimmer would be curious enough to check into my background and find out that I'd been involved in several murders. Maybe if he did, he would dig deep enough to discover that I was the one who had solved those murders, too.

My phone chimed in my pocket. I took it out and saw that Melissa had sent me the information I'd asked for. The email contained a name, Alice Samuels, and a telephone number. I wondered who Alice Samuels was. Probably either Walter's mother or sister, I decided.

While I had the phone out, Detective Zimmer walked up to the verandah. I turned toward him and said, "I've got that name and phone number for you, Detective."

"Thanks." He took out his notebook and wrote down the information. "Do you know how this person is related to Mr. Harvick?"

"No idea." I shared my speculation that Alice Samuels might be Walter's mother or sister.

"Well, I suppose I'll get the job of finding out." Zimmer didn't sound happy about that, and I didn't blame him for feeling that way. Having to notify somebody of a loved one's death had to be a terrible thing to do. Zimmer went on, "I need to ask you a few questions, Tom."

"Sure. I'm glad to help, you know that."

Zimmer looked at Luke and me. "The two of you

can go. But I'd appreciate it if you'd stay here at the resort until I let you know otherwise."

"So my group's scheduled activities are cancelled for the day?" I asked.

"Let's just say they're on hold. It's early yet. We might be able to wrap things up in time for you and your people to go on about your business."

That was the best I could do for the moment, so I nodded and said, "All right, thanks."

Luke and I went into the building, leaving Tom and Zimmer on the verandah. I said, "I want to talk to Mrs. Horton and Mrs. Dunn. They must be really upset."

"Are you sure that detective would want you to do that?" Luke asked with a frown. "They found the body, and he hasn't questioned them yet."

"He didn't tell me not to," I said. "So he can't get upset with me if I do."

Luke looked like he wasn't so sure about that, but he didn't object again. We climbed the stairs and went to the room the two ladies were sharing.

Doris Horton answered my quiet knock. I expected her eyes to be red and puffy from crying, but she looked as calm and composed as could be. She said, "Ms. Dickinson. I suppose you've heard the news."

"That's right," I told her. "How are you and Mrs. Dunn holding up?"

Julia came up to look over Doris's shoulder. She was several inches taller than her friend, so that wasn't any trouble. She said, "We're fine," and looked like she meant it. Like Doris, she didn't appear to have been crying, either.

I began, "I just want you to know that if there's anything I can do – "

"Don't worry, we're all right," Doris said. "Of

course we were upset when it happened, when we saw poor Mr. Harvick lying there – "

"It was Mr. Harvick, wasn't it?" Julia interrupted.

I nodded and said, "I'm afraid so."

"We knew the authorities needed to be notified as soon as possible," Doris went on, "so we hurried right back. But if you thought that seeing him like that would throw us into a tizzy, well, you don't need to worry, Ms. Dickinson. We've seen dead bodies before."

"Sometimes in worse shape than that one," Julia added.

"You have?" Luke burst out. He sounded amazed.

"Oh, yes, certainly," Doris said. "We didn't tell you what our late husbands did for a living, did we?"

I could only shake my head and wonder if the late Mr. Horton and the late Mr. Dunn had been Mafia assassins or something. I'd heard that a lot of mob people retired to Florida just like everybody else.

"They were funeral directors," Doris said.

"Morticians," Julia said.

"They were partners, and since we both worked in the business, too, death was an everyday affair for us."

"Death gave us all a good living, they used to say."

"Funeral director humor."

I had to suppress the impulse to cringe. I didn't want them to see how I really reacted to their comments. So instead I said, "The police are here investigating. I'm sure the detective in charge of the case will want to talk to you."

"We've dealt with the police before," Julia said.

I was glad they had explained about their husbands' business, or else that comment really would've made me suspicious. As it was, I nodded and said, "All right. If I can help you in any way . . ."

"We'll let you know, dear," Doris promised.

She shut the door, and Luke and I didn't say anything as we went back down the hall. When we were well out of earshot, Luke said, "Is it just me, Miz D, or do those two little old ladies seem really creepy now?"

"It's not just you," I told him.

A door opened ahead of us, and crew-cut Phil Thompson came out of the room where he and his wife Sheila were staying. I was a little surprised to see him. With everything that was going on I hadn't really given the matter any conscious thought, but I suppose I'd assumed he was already out on his fishing charter. Most of them left early, before sunrise.

Phil smiled and nodded at us. "Good morning, Ms. Dickinson, Mr. Edwards. You ready to herd the rest of the group around the island again today?"

"There may be a change in plans," I said.

"Oh?" He frowned. "You're not going on with the tour?"

I dodged that question for the moment and said, "I thought you were fishing again today."

"I am. The boat doesn't leave until nine o'clock, though. We're not going as far today, only over to the Dry Tortugas."

I was familiar with that group of islands seventy miles west of here, although I had never been there. A huge, never really completed fort dating back to before the Civil War stood on one of them.

Fort Jefferson was a national monument, partially because it was the southernmost military post on American soil, or at least it had been until it was abandoned in 1874, and partially because Dr. Samuel Mudd, one of the men who'd been convicted of conspiring to assassinate Abraham Lincoln, had been imprisoned there for several years before he was pardoned. The fishing was also supposed to be good around the Dry Tortugas. Hemingway and his Key West friends had gone there frequently to fish, I recalled.

"I'm not sure you'll be able to go," I told Phil Thompson.

His frown deepened. "What? I have to."

"There's been some trouble," I told him with a shake of my head. "The police are here – "

"The police!"

I swear, for a second a look flashed through his eyes that made me think he was going to cut and run for some reason. But then he calmed down and went on, "What's wrong?"

"It looks like Walter Harvick committed suicide down on the beach sometime last night."

"Oh." Phil looked and sounded relieved, but he added quickly, "That's terrible. The poor guy. I don't know why anybody would ever want to do that."

"Me, either," I agreed.

"Did the cops find a note or something?"

As far as I knew, the police hadn't even searched Walter's room yet. If there was a suicide note there, it would certainly simplify matters, I thought.

"I don't know," I told Phil. "We'll just have to wait and see what happens. The detective doesn't want any of us to leave right now."

"Well, that's just – " He stopped and shook his head. "I'm sorry. I don't mean to sound unsympathetic, but I didn't really know the guy, and I've been waiting for a year to get back down here and do some real fishing. You can understand why I'm disappointed."

"Sure," I said, trying to sound sympathetic myself. "Maybe things will be cleared up in time for you to make your trip."

"I hope so. Guess I'd better go let Sheila know what's going on. Looks like she may be stuck having me around today." He turned toward the door of his room, then stopped. "It's all right with the cops if I tell her, isn't it?"

"As far as I know. I don't think they're gonna be able to keep it a secret."

"Not hardly."

When Phil was back in his room, Luke said caustically, "Poor guy. Might have to miss his fishing trip."

"Don't be too hard on him. Like he said, he didn't really know Walter."

But somebody else did, and there was something I was really starting to wonder about, even worry about.

Where was Ronnie Scanlon?

Chapter 13

I had told Detective Zimmer about the little romance going on between Walter and Ronnie, but I hadn't mentioned the fact that Ronnie had been with Walter the last time I saw him. Nor had Zimmer asked about that, probably because despite those detective instincts he had claimed, he wasn't really taking this case seriously as a possible murder. How could he, given the circumstances?

But the more I thought about it, the more concerned I was about Ronnie. Had something happened between them that drove Walter to kill himself?

A wild thought crossed my mind. What if they'd had another argument, and it had escalated to the point that Walter had killed Ronnie? The remorse he would have felt because of that, not to mention the possibility of going to prison, might well have been enough to prompt his suicide.

Or what if they had made some sort of crazed lover's pact to end their lives? Was Ronnie lying somewhere dead on the island, her body not yet discovered?

"Miz D, you're lookin' kinda wild-eyed," Luke said, breaking into my grisly speculations. "Is something wrong? I mean, other than the obvious?"

"No, I was just thinkin' about Ronnie Scanlon," I told him. "You haven't seen her this morning, have you?"

He shook his head. "Nope. I haven't seen her since last night, before I headed for that poker game. She said she was going to stay in and read."

I closed my eyes, reached up, and rubbed my forehead for a second. Luke didn't know yet what had happened the night before in Old Town. As we stood on the balcony, looking down on the lobby, I told him, quickly sketching in the details of running into Walter at Sloppy Joe's while I was with Rollie Cranston.

"So after all that," I concluded, "I left Walter and Ronnie at Captain Tony's. That was the last time I saw either of them."

"So maybe . . . Oh, crap! You think she killed him?"

"Or maybe he killed her," I said, giving voice to the theory that had gone through my head a few minutes earlier. "Or maybe . . ."

"Of course she could be in her room," Luke said when I couldn't go on.

Well, that was so obvious I could have kicked myself. I turned away from the balcony railing and said, "Let's go find out."

"Are you sure that cop won't mind?" Luke asked as he hurried after me.

I fell back on my handy, all-purpose excuse. "He didn't say not to."

I marched straight to the door of Ronnie's room and knocked. There was no answer. I tried the knob. Locked.

Those results didn't do a blasted thing to ease my mind. I said, "Maybe I'd better try to find Detective Zimmer. The police can do a whole lot better job of searching for Ronnie than you and I can. They've got the manpower."

"Yeah, but there's somewhere else we ought to try first," Luke said.

"Where's that?"

"Uh . . . Walter's room?"

Luke reddened as he said it. I figured he could be married to Melissa for thirty years and still blush any time he said anything the least bit racy or suggestive around me. That was sweet, I thought. And he was right, of course. We didn't need to give up and go to the police until we had checked Walter's room. It was possible that Ronnie had spent the night there.

I led the way, and when we reached the door, I rapped my knuckles sharply against it. There was no response right away, so I knocked again. My spirits sank as silence continued on the other side of the door. It looked like Ronnie wasn't here after all, and I was back to worrying about where she was and what might have become of her.

Then the chain rattled as somebody unfastened it, and I was so tense that the sound made me jump a little.

The deadbolt *thunked*, and then the door swung open. Ronnie Scanlon peered out at us. Her hair was a wild tangle, her face was puffy, and the eyes she blinked rapidly at us in confusion were bloodshot, but she was alive, no doubt about that.

"Wha' . . . wha' do you want?" she asked in a voice husky with sleep. "Wha' time's it?"

She had opened the door only a few inches.

115

That was enough of a gap for me to see her bare shoulders. She had wrapped the sheet around herself when she climbed out of bed. You see people do that on TV and in the movies, but I'd never done it in my life. Obviously it did happen in real life from time to time, though, and Ronnie was proof of that.

"Ms. Scanlon . . . Ronnie . . . are you all right?" I asked.

She frowned. "I'm fine. Why wouldn't I be?"

"What happened last night between you and Walter?"

She drew herself up and gave me what she must have hoped was a haughty stare. The tangled hair and generally dissipated look sort of worked against that, though.

"I don't think that's any of your business," she managed to say.

"Maybe not, but it's police business," I said.

"Police . . . police business? I don't understand . . ."

Heavy footsteps on the stairs made me glance around. Luke must have looked, too, because he muttered, "Uh-oh."

Detective Charles Zimmer was coming up the stairs, followed by one of the uniformed officers, and since we could see him, that meant he could see us, too. Judging by the frown on his face, he wasn't happy to find us talking to Ronnie Scanlon.

"What's going on here?" Ronnie asked. She was starting to wake up more now. "Something's wrong. Where's Walter?"

Zimmer reached the top of the stairs and started toward us. "Is that Ms. Scanlon?" he asked in his rumbling voice.

"Who is that man?" Ronnie demanded, adding

116

again, "Where's Walter?"

I would have told her if Zimmer hadn't been right there. As it was, I said, "Ronnie, this is Detective Zimmer."

"Detective . . . Oh, my God! Something's happened to Walter!" She threw the door wide open and rushed out, trailing the bedsheet behind her. "What is it? Where is he?"

Zimmer took out his badge and showed it to her. "Ms. Scanlon, please calm down," he said. "I'm with the Key West Police Department. There's been an incident – "

"It's Walter, isn't it? Something's happened to him!"

"I'm afraid Mr. Harvick is dead."

There's no easy way to fell somebody something like that. The news hit Ronnie like a physical blow, making her grimace and pull back. She let go of the sheet and started to bring her hands to her face in horror. Instinct made her grab the sheet again and gather it around her with one hand while the other covered her eyes.

"No!" she wailed. "No!"

Some people might have thought she was over-doing it. I didn't. Her reaction struck me as gen-uine, and I like to think that I'm a pretty good judge of people, being around as many of them as I am.

"You weren't aware of what happened to Mr. Harvick?" Zimmer asked.

"No! God, no! I still don't know what happened to him, just that you said he . . . he's dead!"

The instinct to protect one of my clients welled up in me. I said, "Look, Detective, you shouldn't be talkin' to Ms. Scanlon while she's standin' here wrapped in a sheet. Can't you at least let her get dressed first?"

He shot a sharp glance at me, as if to ask if I was telling him how to do his job. But he gave one of his minuscule shrugs and said, "I suppose that wouldn't hurt anything. Is this your room, Ms. Scanlon?"

Ronnie had started to sob, so I answered for her. "This is Mr. Harvick's room."

"All right, then maybe she'd better not go back in there. Why don't you take her back to her own room and let her get dressed."

"She'll have to get her room key," I pointed out.

Zimmer thought about it and nodded. He watched Ronnie like a hawk as she fumbled her room key out of her purse.

"The two of you meet me in Mr. Bradenton's office," he said to me she was doing that. "He's a-greed to let me use it for a little while."

"We can do that," I said.

"But don't say anything else to her about what happened," Zimmer warned me quietly in a stern voice.

I nodded.

Zimmer turned to Luke. "I haven't talked to you yet, have I? You're . . .?"

"Luke Edwards," he answered. "Ms. Dickinson's assistant."

"Well, you come on with me, then," Zimmer said to Luke as Ronnie stepped back out of Walter's room.

They headed downstairs while I put an arm around her shoulders and steered her toward her room. Between sobs, she said, "Why . . . why won't he just tell me . . . what happened?"

"You probably heard the detective. I'm not supposed to say anything else."

"But it's bad, though, isn't it? Really bad?"

"Just get some clothes on," I told her. "We'll go down and talk to him."

Zimmer hadn't told me to go into Ronnie's room with her and watch while she got dressed, so I stayed in the hall outside the door, which I left open a crack. I didn't think it was very likely she'd try to climb out the window and make a getaway, but if she did I was hoping I'd hear it and be able to stop her.

Nothing like that happened. She came out a few minutes later wearing Bermuda shorts, a sleeveless blouse, and canvas shoes. She had run a brush through her hair but she hadn't removed her smeared make-up from the night before. She looked about as good as anybody could expect under the circumstances, which was not very good at all.

But she wasn't dead, and that was a considerable improvement over what I'd been worried about for a while.

More people were starting to stir. The dining room opened at seven, and the smell of fresh-brewed coffee was in the air, tantalizing me. I tried to ignore it. I wasn't hungry – after what I'd seen on the beach, it might be a while before I had much of an appetite again – but a cup of coffee would have been mighty welcome right about then.

We went into Tom's little office that opened off the lobby. With a couple of big guys like Zimmer and Luke already in there, it seemed pretty crowded. Zimmer sat behind the desk and motioned Ronnie into the chair in front of it. I thought he might tell Luke and me to get out, but since he didn't, we stood behind Ronnie. I rested a hand on her shoulder to give her some strength. When she heard what Zimmer had to say, she'd probably need it.

He began by asking her, "Ms. Scanlon, when was the last time you saw Mr. Harvick?"

"Why do you want to know that?" she asked right back at him. "You said he was dead, not missing."

"Just answer the question, please."

Ronnie took a deep breath. She said, "Last night, upstairs in his room. We came back here after we left Old Town. That handyman Tom can tell you. He let us in."

"Handyman?" Zimmer repeated with a frown. Then he shook his head, apparently realizing that Ronnie didn't know who Tom Bradenton really was. "So you and Mr. Harvick spent the night together?"

Ronnie lifted her chin defiantly. "Why shouldn't we? We're both grown adults."

"I wasn't passing judgment, Ms. Scanlon, just establishing facts. Key West is pretty relaxed about such things."

"Oh. Well, then, yes, Walter and I spent the night together. At least part of it. When I woke up this morning he was gone, and now you tell me that he . . . he's . . ."

I squeezed her shoulder as her voice trailed off. I thought she was going to start crying again, but she brought herself under control.

"So you didn't know when Mr. Harvick got up and left the room?"

Ronnie shook her head. "No, I didn't. We had quite a bit to drink. I guess I was just sound a-sleep." She leaned forward, and her voice was drawn tight with strain and misery as she went on, "Please. You have to tell me what happened to him."

Zimmer hesitated a couple of seconds before answering, "It appears that Mr. Harvick committed suicide. His body was found on the beach this morning. He had been shot with a shotgun."

I was glad that Zimmer didn't go into gruesome detail. Ronnie would be able to fill in enough of the blanks herself when she stopped to think about Walter's obsession with Ernest Hemingway.

She hunched over in the chair, covered her face with her hands, and cried quietly for several moments. We waited in awkward silence, unable to do anything else.

Zimmer's cell phone broke that silence. The distinctive beat of the opening theme from *Dragnet* filled the little room. I looked across the desk at Zimmer and mouthed the word *Really?* He grimaced as he stood up and took the phone from his shirt pocket.

He opened the phone and said, "Yeah, Doc?" It seemed kind of quick for the medical examiner to have already performed an autopsy on Walter, but I didn't know how many dead bodies they normally had in Key West.

Zimmer listened intently. It was hard to tell from that great stone face of his what was going on in his brain, but I got a general sense that he didn't like what he heard.

Finally he said, "You're sure?" Another pause, then, "No, I know you didn't graduate from a mail-order medical school, Doc. All right, thanks."

He closed the phone and stood there. I could almost see the wheels turning in his brain.

Ronnie lifted her tear-streaked face and asked, "Was that something about Walter? What is it?"

"According to the medical examiner, Mr. Harvick didn't commit suicide after all, Ms.

Scanlon," Zimmer said. "This is a murder investigation now."

Chapter 14

I'd like to say that I was surprised by that revelation . . . but I wasn't. Not really. I'd been waiting for that shoe to drop, and hoping that it wouldn't, ever since I'd seen Walter's body lying on the beach.

The news had changed Detective Zimmer's demeanor. He wasn't taking the case only half-seriously anymore. He looked at Luke and me and said, "You two need to leave while I finish talking to Ms. Scanlon."

I stiffened my back and said, "I don't think so."

Zimmer looked at me in surprise, tilted his head a little to the side, and said, "Oh?"

"That's right. I think Ms. Scanlon should have a lawyer here before she says anything else to you."

Ronnie turned to look at me. She seemed confused.

"This is simply an interview," Zimmer said. "Ms. Scanlon isn't being questioned officially."

"Then everything she's already said to you would have to be considered off-limits when it comes to evidence, wouldn't it?"

"Evidence!" Ronnie said. "You don't mean that he thinks I . . . that I would ever . . ."

"Do you happen to be a lawyer, Ms. Dickinson?" Zimmer asked. "Or are you married to one?"

"No to both questions," I told him.

"And yet you seem somewhat familiar with criminal investigation procedure. That's interesting."

"Somewhat familiar," Luke said. "Mister, you just don't know – " He stopped short and looked at me. "I, uh, probably shouldn't have said that, should I, Miz D?"

"It's all right, Luke," I said. "Detective Zimmer is smart enough he would have found out sooner or later." I faced Zimmer and went on, "I've been involved in several murder cases in the past."

"I was a suspect in one of 'em," Luke said with a slight note of pride in his voice, "but Miz D found the real killer."

"Is that so?" Zimmer said. "That's even more interesting. You're some sort of . . . amateur detective, Ms. Dickinson?"

"No, I just happened to figure out some things. You can call Timothy Farraday if you want to. He's an investigator with the Fulton County Sheriff's Department, and he'll vouch for me."

"I might just do that. In the meantime, I'd appreciate it if you wouldn't try to do any detective work on this case."

"I wasn't planning to," I said honestly. "I'd just like to salvage as much of this tour as I can."

"I'm afraid that's going to be pretty difficult for you now. For the time being, everyone who's here at the resort will have to remain here. There won't be any sightseeing until we get this matter cleared up."

Or any fishing, I thought. Phil Thompson was going to be disappointed.

But that was the least of my worries now.

"I need to talk to my boss," Zimmer went on. "Ms. Scanlon, you can go back to your room if you want, or wherever else you'd like as long as you stay on the grounds."

"What about my things that I left in W-Walter's room?" Her voice broke a little with emotion as she said his name.

"They'll have to wait until Mr. Harvick's room has been searched."

"You'll be getting a warrant for that?" I asked.

He gave me a curt nod. "You can count on it."

I wished I knew what the medical examiner had told him about whatever the autopsy had found to indicate that Walter was murdered instead of committing suicide. I figured the chances of Zimmer sharing that information with me were about as good as the chances of it snowing in Key West for Christmas.

I patted Ronnie's shoulder and said, "Come on. Let's get out of here."

She was still so stunned by everything that had happened she was going to do whatever anybody told her to do. She got to her feet and looked at me. "I can't believe he's dead," she said. "Murdered."

"I know. I'm havin' a hard time believin' it, too."

We left Tom's office with Luke trailing us. Tom was across the lobby, talking to a teenage girl who was working behind the desk. When he spotted us emerging from the office, he crossed the room quickly toward us.

"Is this mess all over?" he asked.

"It's just gettin' started," I told him. "Detective Zimmer just got the word from the medical examiner that Walter didn't commit suicide. He was murdered."

Tom's eyebrows rose in shock. "Good Lord!" he muttered. He looked at Ronnie and went on, "Ms. Scanlon, I'm so sorry."

"Th-thank you," she said. She frowned a little. "You're the . . . handyman? The one who let us in?"

"Ronnie," I told her gently, "this is Tom Bradenton. He owns the resort."

"Oh!" she exclaimed. Even as upset as she was about Walter, she looked embarrassed by her mistake. "Mr. Bradenton, I'm so sorry – "

"Please don't worry about it," he told her with a gentle smile. "People take me for the handyman or the gardener all the time. To tell you the truth, I sort of encourage it. If everybody knew I owned the place, I'd get all the complaints."

"Well, I . . . I didn't mean anything by it," Ronnie said.

"Luke, can you take Ms. Scanlon on up to her room?" I asked. "I want to talk to Mr. Bradenton for a minute."

"Sure, Miz D," he said.

"And then I guess you'd better start breaking the news to the other members of the group and let them know that for the time being they're confined to the grounds of the resort."

He nodded without saying anything. I knew I had given him a lousy job. Some of the clients might be sympathetic when they heard about what happened, but others were bound to be upset and angry at having their trip interfered with.

When Luke and Ronnie had gone upstairs, I turned to Tom and said, "I really am sorry about all this. Having a murder take place at your resort is bound to be bad for business."

He stuck his hands in his pockets and said, "Don't be so sure about that. Remember, Key West was founded by wreckers and smugglers. Some of them were pretty unsavory sorts. Given the area's history, there have probably been a lot of murders committed up and down these keys."

"Maybe so. I hate that it had to happen, anyway."

"Do you know what made Charles change his mind about Mr. Harvick's death being suicide?"

I shook my head. "All I know is that the medical examiner called him and told him something. The two of you are friends. Maybe he'd tell you."

"I don't think so," Tom said. "Charles has always been pretty close-mouthed about his work. He's not the sort to gossip."

Given Zimmer's stern demeanor, I could imagine that.

"You mind if I pick your brain about something else?" I asked.

"Sure," Tom agreed readily. "But why don't we go in the dining room and get some coffee first? I don't know about you, but I could sure use some. Then we can sit down and talk."

That sounded good to me, too. I nodded and let him lead the way.

A few people were enjoying the continental breakfast, but none of my clients so far. Tom asked me if I wanted anything to eat, but I shook my head and went straight to the big coffee urn instead. When both of us had filled our cups, we went to the table farthest from anyone else and sat down. It was next to a big window that looked out at a beautiful flower garden. I couldn't help but think about how pleasant it would be just to sit here and enjoy the morning with Tom Bradenton, if it hadn't been for the subject that we had to discuss.

He wrapped his hands around his coffee cup and said, "Before we talk about whatever you wanted to ask me, Delilah, I want to say that I hope you haven't had any regrets about last night. If I was a little too forward – "

"Are you talkin' about that kiss on the beach?" I asked him. "If you are, that was as much my idea as it was yours, Tom, and I haven't regretted it one bit. In fact, I'm pretty danged sure that it's been the highlight of the trip so far."

His mouth quirked. "But under the circumstances, that wouldn't take a whole lot, would it?"

"I think it would have been the highlight of a lot of my trips," I said as I looked across the table at him.

After a moment he cleared his throat and asked, "What was it you wanted to talk to me about?"

"Since you seem to know just about everybody on the island, I figured you could recommend a good lawyer."

"Sure, I – Wait a minute. Are you talking about a lawyer for you? Surely Charles Zimmer doesn't think that you could've had anything to do with Mr. Harvick's death. That's preposterous!"

"Well, I don't have an alibi," I pointed out, "but I don't really have a motive, either. I was thinkin' more about Ronnie Scanlon. From the looks of it, she was the last one to see Walter alive . . . except for the person who killed him."

"And the two of them were romantically involved, you said. Not exactly the same as the spouse always being the primary suspect, but at least in the same neighborhood."

"Yeah. She doesn't have an alibi, either. I just

think Detective Zimmer is gonna put a lot of pressure on her, and she ought to be ready for it."

Tom nodded and said, "I agree. I know several good attorneys. I'll think about it and decide which one would be the best for this. Should I let you know who I decide or just go ahead and contact whoever I pick?"

"If you want to go ahead and call 'em, that would be great," I said.

"Okay. Was there anything else you wanted to ask me?"

I shook my head. "No, that's it. I appreciate your help, and I'm sure Ronnie will, too."

"I haven't done anything yet. But I will." He took a sip of his coffee. "Could I ask you something, real quick?"

"Of course."

"Don't take this the wrong way, but you don't seem to be quite as shaken up by all this as I might have expected. You're very . . . efficient."

I laughed. "Thanks . . . I think. This isn't the first time I've had to deal with something like this during a tour."

"A client dying, you mean?"

"No, I was talking about murder."

He gave me that surprised look again. I didn't figure it would do any harm to tell him. All he had to do was look up my name on the Internet to find some pretty sensationalized newspaper stories.

"I've run into murder before," I went on. "Once at a plantation during a Gone With the Wind tour, on a Mississippi riverboat going through Mark Twain country, and then a while back in New Orleans while I had a group attending the Tennessee Williams Literary Festival."

"That's incredible," he murmured. "And people

still sign up for your tours?" He leaned forward hurriedly. "Wait a minute. I didn't mean that the way it sounded – "

"It's all right," I told him. "You didn't say anything I haven't thought a hundred times. Luckily, most of my tours have been just fine, and it's not like I play up the murders on the agency website. Most of the time, folks don't even know about them."

"Does Charles know about them?"

"Detective Zimmer? Yeah, I told him a little about those other cases."

"Did he warn you not to get involved in trying to solve this one?"

"Not in so many words," I said, "but I don't think he'd like me stickin' my nose in where he thinks it doesn't belong."

"I'm sure he wouldn't," Tom said with a smile. "Charles is a pretty strait-laced sort of guy."

"He doesn't really dress like one," I said, thinking about Zimmer's brightly flowered shirt.

"Trust me, for Key West that's practically a Brooks Brothers suit." Tom drank some more of his coffee and then said, "So, are you?"

"Am I what?"

"Going to try to find out who killed Walter Harvick."

"Key West is nice, but I don't think I want to spend any extra time here in jail. I'm gonna look after my clients, and that's it."

He nodded and said, "That's probably a wise decision. And speaking of looking after your clients, I promised to come up with a good lawyer for Ms. Scanlon. I'll go make some calls."

He got to his feet, and I stood up, too. "Thank you, Tom," I told him. "It helps knowin' I've got one of the locals to lean on."

"Any time," he said. He left the dining room, taking his coffee with him.

I hadn't drunk much of mine yet, so I sat down at the table again and sipped it while I looked out at the flowers, thinking again how pretty it was here. Walter Harvick's death was a reminder, though, that ugliness could always intrude, no matter how beautiful the surroundings.

Footsteps coming toward me made me look around a few minutes later. At first I thought Tom might be back already, but I saw it was Luke crossing the dining room instead.

And from the look on his face, he wasn't bringing me good news.

I stood up to meet him, asking, "What is it, Luke?"

"I started going around to alert folks to what's happened, like you told me to," he said. "I told them the police want them to stay here at the resort. But when I got to the Thompsons' room . . . they're not there, Miz D. I've looked all over for 'em, and they're gone."

Chapter 15

So much for a few minutes of peace and quiet. I stood up and kept my voice low so the other people in the dining room wouldn't overhear as I said, "Maybe they're outside on the grounds somewhere."

Luke shook his head. "I've looked all over. They're not around, and nobody has seen them."

"You're sure they're not in their room?"

"Well . . . nobody came to the door. It was locked, so I couldn't go in. But I called both their cell phones, and nobody answered." He hesitated. "You don't think anything happened to them, do you?"

"We saw Phil a little while ago, and he looked fine then," I reminded him.

"Yeah, I thought about that. You think maybe he took off to go on that fishing trip anyway?"

I considered the question for a second and said, "I wouldn't put it past him. But that doesn't explain where Sheila is."

"Maybe he took her with him."

That was possible, although Sheila had made it plain by her comments about Phil's activities that she didn't care for deep-sea fishing. It didn't explain why neither of them had answered their cell phone, either.

"Come on," I told Luke. "Let's go take another look around."

"Don't you trust me, Miz D?"

"Of course I do, honey, but it never hurts to double-check."

We left the dining room and went upstairs, where I knocked on the door of the Thompsons' room and called through the door, "Phil? Sheila?"

There was no answer, and as Luke had said, the door was locked.

Getting Tom to unlock the door was a last resort – no pun intended – as far as I was concerned, so we went out to check the grounds. We left the beach for last and headed there only when we didn't find any sign of the Thompsons anywhere else.

I didn't think the beach would be open, and sure enough, yellow crime scene tape was strung from tree to tree all along the edge of it, putting the sand off-limits except for several people who were puttering around the area where Walter's body had been found. They wore khaki shorts and blue t-shirts that had the word POLICE on the back, plus there were several briefcases and various bags sitting around, so I assumed they were crime scene investigators.

The overall emptiness of the beach made it easy to see that the Thompsons weren't there. Luke stood beside me and asked glumly, "Now what?"

"We can either go tell Detective Zimmer that they're gone, or we can get Tom Bradenton to let us into their room."

"What if they're in there . . . well, you know?"

"Foolin' around?" I said, even though I knew that's not what he meant at all.

"Murdered," Luke said.

"Then it would be better for Zimmer to find 'em, not us. Come on."

"You're going to talk to the detective?"

"I'll protect my clients all I can without gettin' you or me into trouble with the law," I said. "But Phil knew good and well that everybody was supposed to stay here at the resort until they were told otherwise. If he took Sheila and snuck off, that trouble's on his head . . . especially if it was just to go fishin'."

Luke didn't argue with that sentiment. We walked back through the trees and along the crushed coral path to the main house.

I thought we'd probably find Detective Zimmer in Tom's office, and sure enough, that's where he was, talking on his cell phone. The door was open halfway, so I stuck my head in. When he saw me, he held up a blunt finger in the universal signal to wait a minute.

He finished his conversation – from the sound of it he was talking to one of his superiors – and closed the phone. "What can I do for you, Ms. Dickinson?"

"I had my associate Mr. Edwards inform all of my clients that they're confined to the grounds for the time bein'," I told him. "I figure you've got officers posted to keep folks here . . ."

"I do," he said with a nod.

"But I thought it would be helpful if we gave them a heads-up about what's goin' on."

"Spread the word about the murder, you mean?" he rumbled at me.

Luke spoke up, saying, "I didn't tell them any-

135

thing about that, sir. I just said there was a police situation and that they couldn't leave right now."

Zimmer nodded slowly. "Well, fine," he said. "I suppose that didn't hurt anything."

"The thing of it is," I said, "a couple of my clients don't seem to be here anymore."

He sat up sharply. "Not here? Where are they?"

"I don't know. But Luke and I have double-checked the whole place, and they're gone."

"Who?" Zimmer snapped. "Is Ms. Scanlon one of them?"

He was probably just aching to put out an APB on her. With her being the last known person to see Walter, if she fled on top of that he'd be convinced that she was guilty. So I was glad to say, "No, it's not Ronnie. Phil and Sheila Thompson are the ones who are missing."

He frowned and glanced at a sheet of paper in front of him on the desk. I wondered if it was a list of my clients. "Thompson," he muttered. "That's the guy who went deep-sea fishing yesterday, instead of to the Hemingway House and Old Town, right?"

"Right," I said. "He was supposed to go out on a charter today, too, but I told him he couldn't."

"So you have seen Phil Thompson today?"

I glanced at the clock on the wall of Tom's office. "Yeah, about an hour and a half ago. That was before you knew that Walter was murdered, while you were still treatin' the case as a likely suicide."

"And while we weren't being quite as vigilant about keeping track of where everybody was," Zimmer said with a scowl.

"So Phil could've gotten his wife and slipped away?"

"They're not here, according to you, so that must be what happened."

Zimmer's attitude was starting to annoy me a little. It wasn't my fault that Phil and Sheila had taken off somewhere.

"How did Harvick get along with the Thompsons?" he continued.

"I'm not sure they said a dozen words to each other during the whole trip. I'm not even sure they knew each other's names."

"Were the Thompsons around when Harvick had his trouble with other people?"

"They were at Sloppy Joe's the first night," I said. "The entire group went. I don't know if they saw what happened between Walter and Rollie Cranston, though. Phil didn't go to the Hemingway House yesterday, and I'm pretty sure Sheila was in the gift shop when Walter had his run-ins there." I ventured an opinion. "I can't see any reason to think they might be connected with Walter's murder. They didn't really have anything to do with him."

"And yet they're gone," Zimmer said.

"And yet they're gone," I agreed.

He sighed. "All right, thanks for letting me know. Can you give me descriptions of them?"

"So you can put out APBs on them?"

"I'm not sure we have to go quite that far just yet. But I would like to circulate their descriptions to the officers on the island."

"Sure. They're both in their forties, I'd say. Phil's got light brown hair, and he wears it in a crew-cut."

Zimmer looked surprised. "Really? A crew-cut?" He pointed. "The Bermuda Triangle and the wormhole leading back to 1957 are that way."

That was more of a joke than I expected from him, certainly under the circumstances. At least I hoped it was a joke.

He poised his pen over his notebook and said, "Go on."

"I guess he's about six feet, weighs one-eighty." I looked at Luke. "You agree with that?"

"On the height, yeah," he said. "I've never been good at all at guessing how much somebody weighs."

"Phil's retired from the military, but I don't know which branch," I told Zimmer. "Maybe that explains the crew-cut. He teaches algebra in high school. Sheila teaches English in their local junior high. She has blond hair, sort of curly. I'd say she's five-five or five-six. Weighs maybe a hundred and forty."

"She's not going to stand out in a crowd," Zimmer said, "but it sounds like her husband might. You told me he chartered Jimmy Malone's boat to go fishing yesterday?"

"You're the one who mentioned Mr. Malone's name," I reminded him. "All I knew was the name of the boat."

Zimmer nodded. "I'll check the marina where Jimmy anchors. If he's not there, maybe Thompson went out with him again and dragged his wife along this time. Is the guy single-minded enough to do that even though he was told to stay put?"

I thought about that for a moment and then said, "He probably is. He seemed really disappointed when Luke and I told him he couldn't go out today."

"Then that's the most likely explanation. Still, I'm going to send out their descriptions and ask our patrol officers to keep an eye out for them."

Luke asked, "Are they going to be in trouble when you catch them?"

"That depends on why they snuck out of here,"

Zimmer said. "If they're running away from a murder charge . . . yeah, they'll be in trouble."

That still seemed pretty far-fetched to me, but I knew better than to think that it just wasn't possible.

"We'll let you go on about your business," I told Zimmer.

"Thanks again for the heads-up."

We left the office, and as we walked across the lobby, Luke asked, "What do we do now?"

"There's not much we can do except wait," I said.

Behind us, someone said, "Ms. Dickinson?"

Not recognizing the voice and not knowing what to expect, I felt a little tingle of apprehension as Luke and I stopped and turned around. I had been in enough of these situations to know that no matter how bad they were, there was usually a way for them to get even worse.

Chapter 16

The man who had spoken to me didn't look particularly threatening, though. He was in his twenties and wore a lightweight, rather rumpled cream-colored suit. His tie was a sunburst red. He was carrying around an extra fifty pounds, so in this heat and humidity the flushed look on his face was probably the next thing to permanent. His brown beard was a little ragged, his already thinning hair slightly askew. He had a briefcase in his left hand. He thrust out his right and said again, "Ms. Dickinson?"

"I'm Delilah Dickinson," I confirmed.

"I thought you must be." He gave me a smile that was part leer. "Mr. Bradenton told me to look for a gorgeous redhead. I'm Pete Nickleby." He added, "Attorney at law."

I took his hand. His palm was a little sweaty, just like I expected it to be. As I let go of it, I inclined my head toward Luke and said, "This is my associate, Luke Edwards."

Nickleby gave Luke a quicker handshake than I'd gotten and a perfunctory "Pleased to meetcha."

Then he set his briefcase on the floor at his feet and pointed both index fingers at me. "Mr. Bradenton says you're a tour guide and one of your tourists killed somebody or somethin', right?"

While I was trying not to gape at him and trying even harder to come up with an answer to that, a more familiar voice said, "Pete, is that you? What are you doing here?"

Nickleby turned his head and said, "Oh, hiya, Mr. Bradenton. I'm here about that murder case."

Tom looked a little pained as he came up to us. "Keep your voice down, Pete. I'm sure there's already plenty of gossip going around about what happened, but we don't need to add to it."

"Oh, yeah, right. Discretion. I'm the soul of it." He looked at me again. "So where's the killer?"

"Hold on a minute." Tom took hold of Nickleby's arm and turned him toward the doors. "Let's all go outside where we can talk in private."

"Fine by me, but it's hot out there already. Gonna be a scorcher. You got good A/C in here, you know that, Mr. Bradenton?"

Luke and I looked at each other and then followed along as Tom steered Pete Nickleby toward the doors. If he was the best lawyer Tom could come up with, the legal situation on Key West must have been a lot worse than I thought.

Tom led us into the garden, to a secluded nook among the flower beds and palm trees. He said, "What are you doing here, Pete? I thought your father was coming."

"Dad's out of town," Nickleby answered. "Didn't the phone girl tell you? I'm handling things until he gets back."

"I did not know that," Tom said slowly. "When are you expecting Edward?"

"Gee, I dunno. He's up in Miami on a big case. Probably not gonna wrap up until next week sometime."

"Okay. Listen, Pete, I'm not sure this is a good idea – "

"I can handle it, Mr. Bradenton, I swear." For a second Pete Nickleby looked more like a puppy eager to please than he did the sleazeball he had come off as earlier. "If you let me take care of this for you, it'll really impress my dad, what with you and him being friends. And I'm actually a pretty good lawyer, you know. Forty-seventh in my class."

"It's not up to me," Tom told him. He looked at me. "What do you think, Delilah?"

Before I could answer, Nickleby leaned closer to Tom, lowered his voice, and said, "You were right, ya know. She is smokin' hot."

I had to grit my teeth a little as I said, "Tom, can I talk to you?"

"Sure." He told Pete, "You wait right here," and once again I was reminded of a puppy. Tom might as well have said, "Sit."

We moved off about twenty feet up the path, and in a half-whisper Tom said, "Just for the record, that's not the way I described you. Not that you're not – "

I waved that off and asked quietly, "Is he really the best lawyer that Key West has to offer?"

"No, but his father is. Edward Nickleby is top tier all the way."

"Except maybe genetically," I said.

"Here's the thing," Tom went on. "If Ms. Scanlon winds up charged with murder, then it would be good to have Edward's firm in her corner, not to mention Edward himself. All you need Pete for right now is to make sure that she has some represent-tation. He's pretty goofy, but he ought to be able to handle things as long as they don't get too complicated, and his dad can take over when he gets back next week." He paused and shook his head ruefully. "But I swear that when I talked to the receptionist, she didn't tell me she would be sending Pete over here."

I sighed and said, "All right. I suppose if it means getting a good law firm on retainer for Ronnie in case things go bad, we can put up with him for a while."

With that settled, we went back to join Luke and Pete, who was talking at what seemed to be his usual mile-a-minute pace, telling Luke some story about college coeds on spring break, a llama, and a giant cardboard cutout of Yoda. I didn't want to hear the details.

"All right, Mr. Nickleby," I told him when he paused to take a breath, "we've decided to retain your services on behalf of Ms. Veronica Scanlon . . . if, of course, she agrees to that as well."

"Great! She's the murderer?"

"No, we don't think so," I said, trying to hang on to my patience. "But that's why she needs a lawyer. She was the last person to see the victim – "

"Then she must've bumped him off, right?"

"Pete," Tom said sternly, "be quiet and listen, all right?"

"Oh, yeah, sure." Pete gave me that half-leer smile again and said in a confidential tone, "I tend to get carried away."

"As I was sayin' . . . Ronnie was the last person to see Walter Harvick that we know of."

"Harvick's the dead guy?"

"Yes. Someone killed him with a shotgun and tried to make it look like suicide."

"Oh!" Pete's eyes opened wider. "The ol' Papa Hemingway bit. Blew his head up like a pumpkin dropped from the roof of the Ed Sullivan Theater, right?"

Luke growled. An actual growl. I put a hand on his arm, took a deep breath, and went on, "Ronnie and Walter were spendin' the night in Walter's room in the main house. Sometime durin' the night, Walter got up and slipped out without wakin' Ronnie. After that, he wound up on the beach, dead."

Pete got a thoughtful look on his face and said, "You know, I don't really like the idea of giving chicks guys' names. Like, there are actresses named Michael and James. That's nuts. But I guess Ronnie's not too bad. That's what Archie called Veronica, after all."

Tom said, "Let's stick to the case, Pete."

"Oh, yeah, yeah, sorry." His frown deepened. He pointed his fingers at me again. "Okay, serious now. If this Ronnie girl was the last one to see the victim alive, and she doesn't have an alibi – she doesn't, right?"

"That's right," I said.

"Then the cops are gonna take her in and hold her for questioning, at the very least. That's where I come in." He made an emphatic gesture. "I'm gonna be sitting right there beside her telling her not to answer any of their questions."

"Won't that look suspicious?" Luke asked.

Pete waved a hand. "Doesn't matter. Let 'em be suspicious. How many cases have there been where, gee, everybody and his *dog* knows who the real killer was, but the police never make an arrest because they have 'insufficent evidence'." I could hear the quote marks around the last two words.

"The important thing is keeping the client out of jail."

"I thought the important thing was justice," Luke said.

Pete gave him an indulgent smile. "Yeah, well, you didn't go to law school, did you, pal?" He turned back to me. "Okay, I need to talk to the client, go through her story, make sure I've got everything straight, as the actress said to the bishop. Where is she?"

I hated to admit it, but I had sort of lost track of where Ronnie was. I was sure she had to be here at the resort somewhere.

"Let's try her room," I said.

"And Pete, you need to be on your best behavior," Tom added.

"Of course." Pete squared his shoulders, straightened his tie, and swiped at his suit as if he were trying to brush out some of the wrinkles. He didn't have much luck with that.

We hadn't quite reached the front doors of the main house when Detective Zimmer came out through them. He stopped short, looked at Pete, and said, "Counselor."

"Oh, hey, Detective," Pete greeted him.

"You're not representing Ms. Scanlon, are you?"

"Yes, indeedy. If she'll have me." Pete closed one eye in an elaborate wink. "And most women are good to go along with that, if you know what I mean."

Zimmer looked like he was trying hard not to laugh. He said, "I'll be back later. All of you hold yourselves available for interviews."

"Sure. We'll hold ourselves."

Zimmer said, "I wasn't including you in that, counselor. But I'm sure you'll be around anyway."

Zimmer gave Tom a look and walked off.

I thought it was probably a look of pity.

The four of us went into the house. I saw right away that I was in for trouble. All the members of my group, with the exceptions of the Thompsons, Ronnie, and of course Walter, were sitting around the lobby, talking. They saw us come in. George Matheson, Frank Cleburne, and Matt Altman all popped up from their chairs and hurried toward me.

George took the lead. He said, "Ms. Dickinson, the cops say we can't leave the resort."

"That's right," I replied. "Luke came around and explained to you – "

"He didn't say what it's all about," Frank cut in. "There's a rumor going around that somebody was killed. Maybe that Walter guy."

"The one who gave me trouble," Matt added. "Is it true, Ms. Dickinson?"

I wasn't going to lie to them. I nodded and said, "Yes, Walter Harvick was murdered last night."

"Oh, man," Matt said, his eyes widening until it looked like they were going to pop out of their sockets. "No wonder that cop was asking me and Aimee all those questions!"

Pete looked at me and asked, "Is this another potential killer?"

"I didn't kill anybody!" Matt exclaimed. "Ms. Dickinson, who's this guy?"

"Take it easy, Mr. Altman," I told him without answering his question about Pete Nickleby. "Nobody's accusing you of anything. Were you and your wife together all night?"

"Now you're asking me for an alibi!"

"No, no, settle down. I'm just tryin' to get everything – " I started to say "straight", but then remembered Pete's comment a few minutes earlier and didn't see any point in setting him up for that joke again. "Squared away," I finished.

"Well, Aimee and I were together in our cottage all night," Matt said. "I didn't set foot out of it until this morning. Is that a good enough alibi?"

"It sounds fine to me," I said.

"Did the cop believe it?" Pete asked.

Matt frowned. "I still don't know who you are."

"Come on, Mr. Nickleby," I said. I'd gotten Pete here to represent Ronnie. He couldn't represent any of my other clients without it being a conflict of interest.

I hoped I wouldn't have to scrounge up lawers for all of them before this was over.

We went up the stairs. Pete was puffing pretty hard from that extra weight of his by the time we reached the top. He had to stop to catch his breath. He held up a hand, palm out, and motioned for us to wait.

"I'm okay," he said a few moments later. "Gotta get back to the gym soon."

He didn't look like he'd ever set foot in a gym, but I could have been wrong about that. When he had recovered from climbing the stairs, we went along the balcony to Ronnie's room. Walter's room, several doors down, was sealed off with the ubiquitous yellow tape.

I knocked on the door and called her name, adding, "It's Delilah Dickinson."

She didn't answer. It was possible she was somewhere else in the house or on the grounds, but since I hadn't seen her in the lobby with the others, I'd sort of expected to find her here. I knocked again and still got no response.

"I can unlock the door if you want," Tom offered.

"Maybe it's open," I said as I reached down to try the knob.

For a change, the door actually was unlocked. The knob turned as I grasped it. I pushed the door open.

Then stepped back and gasped, because I could see into the room and what I saw was Ronnie Scanlon lying face down on the bed, utterly motionless.

Chapter 17

Tom shouldered past me and rushed into the room. Luke was right behind him. Pete Nickleby stayed outside the door with me and muttered, "Holy cow! Another murder!"

If he had added something about this being so cool, I would have turned and slugged him. Luckily, he didn't.

We were all going to feel foolish if it turned out that Ronnie was just sound asleep. Something about the limp way she was lying there told me that wasn't the case, though.

Tom bent over the bed and felt her neck, searching for a pulse. After a moment he looked up at me and nodded.

"She's alive," he said, and those two words made relief rush through me. "It looks like she's not in good shape, though."

Ronnie hadn't stirred when Tom checked her pulse. He rolled her onto her back, jogged her shoulder a couple of times, and even lightly slapped her face, but he got the same lack of response.

"She must have taken something," he said. "We'd better get an ambulance here right away."

"Or she was poisoned!" Pete exclaimed, and although I already hated to agree with anything he said, he wasn't saying anything I hadn't already thought of myself.

Tom had his phone out. He got through to 911 right away and asked for an ambulance to be sent to the main house of the Bradenton Beach Resort. As he closed his phone and put it away, I thought that Detective Zimmer, whatever he was doing at the moment, was liable to hear about that call and come rushing back here to see what was going on.

"Give me a hand, Luke," Tom said. "Let's get her on her feet. She needs to be up and moving around, even if she's unconscious. That'll get the blood flowing better."

"Are you sure we should move her any more than we already have?" Luke asked. "We don't want to make the situation worse."

"If we let her sink any farther, she might not come out of it."

I didn't know if Tom was right or not, but what he was saying seemed to make sense. I said, "Go ahead, Luke. I think it's the best thing to do."

"Okay, Miz D." He got on one side of Ronnie and Tom got on the other, and together they lifted her from the bed and set her on her feet. Her muscles were limp so her legs wouldn't support her, but they began carrying her around the room, making her legs move back and forth.

After they had been doing that for a few minutes, Ronnie stirred a little. Her head had been hanging forward, but she lifted it slightly and shook it slowly from side to side. Once to the right, once to the left. She moaned softly.

"Come on, Ms. Scanlon," Luke urged. "You've got to wake up."

Ronnie didn't say anything.

I heard sirens somewhere outside. They seemed to be coming closer.

A minute later there was no doubt about it. The wailing noise got louder and then stopped. I turned and looked down into the lobby. A couple of EMTs wearing shorts and t-shirts – the official uniform of every public servant in Key West, it seemed like – hurried in carrying their lifesaving gear.

"Up here!" I called to them, and when they looked up at the balcony I waved.

They didn't waste any time taking over. While one of them checked Ronnie's vitals after Tom and Luke lowered her back onto the bed, the other one talked to me and got the story.

"She seems to be relatively stable," the first one reported.

"We'll get her in the ambulance and pump her stomach," the second one decided. He looked at me again. "Was this an accidental overdose or deliberate?"

"Does that matter right now?" I asked.

He gave me a grim smile. "Not really. I'll go get the gurney." He looked at Tom. "You've got an elevator here, don't you, Mr. Bradenton?"

"Yeah, had to put it in to comply with ADA," Tom said. "I'll show you."

I hadn't noticed an elevator in the main house while we were there, so I supposed it was tucked into an out-of-the-way corner.

Tom and the second EMT hurried off. The one sitting on the bed next to Ronnie said to Luke, Pete, and me, "You folks need to step back out of the way. We'll take care of the lady."

Luke was the only one of us actually in the room. Pete Nickleby and I were still standing just outside the door. Luke joined us and we all moved back far enough that they could get in with the gurney when it got here, but I stayed where I could keep an eye on Ronnie.

"This your second trip out here today?" Pete asked the EMT.

"That's right. How'd you know?"

Pete pointed at Ronnie and said, "She's a suspect in the murder that happened earlier. I'm her lawyer."

"Is that so?"

"Somebody blew a guy's head off, eh? I'll bet that was pretty ugly."

"I've seen worse," the EMT said. He seemed to be getting a little impatient with Pete's chatter. I had a hunch Pete affected a lot of people that way.

"Both barrels in the mouth. Man, what a way to go. I guess you wouldn't really feel it much, though. And there sure wouldn't be much chance of lingering, would there?"

"No, not really," the EMT said.

"Of course, that's if you're committing suicide. This guy was murdered, or so I'm told. You know anything about that?"

"Not my job to know anything about that," the EMT replied curtly. "I just try to keep the live ones alive and tote the dead ones."

His tone made it clear that he didn't want to continue the conversation. That was all right because a few minutes later Tom and the other EMT came back with the gurney. It didn't take long to get Ronnie loaded up and wheeled out of the room. They took her off around a corner to the elevator while Tom, Luke, Pete, and I went down the stairs.

Detective Charles Zimmer came through the front doors just as we reached the bottom of the stairs. He was hurrying, and I took that as confirmation that my earlier guess was right. He'd heard the emergency call, or someone had told him about it, and he wanted to find out what was happening here at his crime scene.

Zimmer put out a hand toward us and said, "All of you hold it right there."

Pete said, "That's what she – Oof!"

Luke had elbowed him in the side to shut him up.

"Why was there an ambulance call to this address?" Zimmer asked. "Is someone else hurt?"

"We found Ms. Scanlon unconscious in her room," Tom explained. "It looked to me like she had overdosed on something."

"Tried to kill herself?"

Tom shrugged. "You'll have to ask her about that, once she's conscious again."

"If she lives," Pete added.

I gave him a dirty look, then said to Zimmer, "Don't jump to any conclusions, Detective."

"I don't jump to conclusions, Ms. Dickinson. I arrive at them logically. And logic, as well as experience, tells me that a suicide attempt is often a sign of a guilty conscience."

"Or grief," I said. "It can be motivated by grief at losing a loved one, too."

"Ms. Scanlon knew Walter Harvick for less than two days," Zimmer pointed out. "That's not really long enough to consider him a loved one."

Luke said, "Haven't you ever heard of love at first sight, Detective?"

Zimmer grunted. "Heard of it. Don't believe in

it."

"Well . . . well, maybe you should."

With a creaking of rubber wheels, the gurney rolled into the lobby. The EMTs pointed it toward the door. One of them nodded to Zimmer and said, "Detective."

"An officer's going to follow you to the hospital to keep an eye on Ms. Scanlon," Zimmer said.

"That's fine."

"How's she look?"

"I think she'll be all right, but don't quote me on that."

They went on out. Zimmer lingered, looking at us as he asked, "Did Ms. Scanlon say anything to any of you to indicate that she might be planning to do away with herself?"

"Not to me," I said, and Luke shook his head.

"Hey, I never even talked to her yet," Pete said. "But don't forget, she's still my client. Provisionally."

"Then maybe you'd better go to the hospital, too, counselor, and look after her best interests."

"Yeah, that's a good idea." Pete looked at me. "I'm still hired, right?"

"Go," I told him. He hustled out of the lobby, circling wide around Zimmer, who stood rooted like a tree.

When Pete was gone, Zimmer said, "The rest of you will have to stay here. This doesn't change anything. The investigation is still going on."

Quite a few people were in the lobby. The sirens had drawn them out of their rooms. Some were members of my group, but not all of them. A man who was a stranger to me said, "How long are we going to be stuck here, Officer?"

The woman who was with him said, "Yes, we

shouldn't even have to stay here. We're not part of the murder group."

Murder group. Hearing it phrased like that made my heart sink a little. If the things that had happened before hadn't ruined my business, this trip was bound to.

"I'm sorry," Zimmer told the couple. "We're proceeding as fast as we can. Everyone here at the resort, guests and staff alike, will have to be interviewed before anyone can be allowed to leave."

"Then don't you think you should get some more cops busy at that?" another man asked.

"Our department has limited resources," Zimmer said. "We've had cutbacks like everybody else."

I didn't doubt that. And since there were quite a few people here at the resort, it would take a while to talk to all of them, as Zimmer had said.

There were other complaints from the crowd, but Zimmer ignored them. He looked at Luke and me and said, "Come on. I need to talk to you. All right to keep using your office, Tom?"

"Sure," Tom replied. "Anything to help out and get things back to normal around here."

I didn't know what Zimmer wanted now, but there was only one way to find out. Luke and I followed him into Tom's office. He motioned for Luke to close the door.

Zimmer didn't sit down behind the desk and didn't invite us to sit, either. He jammed his hands into the pockets of his shorts and said, "You told me Phil Thompson chartered the *Mary Lou* to go deep-sea fishing yesterday."

I frowned. "That's what he told me. Have you found the Thompsons?"

"You're sure it couldn't have been some other boat?"

"I don't think so," I answered honestly. "I'm pretty sure it was the *Mary Lou.*"

"Why would he tell you which boat he was taking out?" Zimmer wanted to know.

"Shoot, I don't know." I was surprised and a little confused by these questions. "He just mentioned it in passing while we were talking on the way down here in the van, day before yesterday. He was saying how much he enjoyed fishing, and his wife Sheila said that was all he really enjoyed doing, and he said . . . No, wait. Sheila mentioned the boat first. She said she'd rather Phil be out on a boat with a girl's name instead of running around with a real girl. And that's when Phil said the boat was called the *Mary Lou.* I got the name right, Detective."

Zimmer nodded slowly. "I had a feeling that you did. I went to see Jimmy Malone a little while ago. He's the one who owns that boat."

"He wasn't out with the Thompsons today?"

"He wasn't out with Phil Thompson yesterday," Zimmer said. "According to Jimmy, he never even heard of Phil or Sheila Thompson, and neither had any of the other charter boat skippers in the marina. I went around and asked all of them, just to be sure." Zimmer fixed me with a hard stare. "Whatever Phil Thompson came to Key West for, it wasn't the fishing."

Chapter 18

Well, I was flabbergasted by that. The Thompsons had seemed like such nice, normal people. It was obvious they'd been lying to me, though, and whatever they were up to, they were both in on it. Sheila had set me up for Phil to tell me the name of the boat he had supposedly chartered. She wouldn't have done that if she hadn't been helping him plant his lie.

"You don't know anything about this?" Zimmer pressed.

"Not a blasted thing. I've told you everything I know, Detective."

Zimmer didn't say anything for several seconds, as if he was trying to decide whether to believe me. Then he said, "All right. I'm going let the chief know to step up the search for them. If you hear anything from either of them, I expect you to get in touch with me right away."

"I will," I promised.

Zimmer looked at Luke. "The same goes for you, Mr. Edwards."

He nodded and said, "Of course, Detective."

Looking even grumpier than usual, Zimmer strode out of the office, leaving the door open behind him. Luke looked over at me and said, "What do you think is going on, Miz D?"

All I could do was shake my head and say, "I don't have any earthly idea. It looks like Detective Zimmer considers Phil and Sheila suspects in Walter's murder, though."

"That doesn't make any sense! Why would they kill him? They barely knew him."

That was true, but my brain was turning over pretty quickly and putting a few things together. To help me think it through, I said, "Whatever Phil and Sheila came to Key West to do, they wanted to keep it a secret. That's why they came up with that story about deep-sea fishing. It wouldn't take but a few minutes on the Internet to find the name of a boat Phil could pretend to charter. He didn't figure anybody would ever check up on him. There wouldn't have been any reason to . . . if Walter hadn't been killed."

"So it would have made more sense for them *not* to kill Walter," Luke pointed out. "That just drew attention to them."

"Maybe they didn't have any choice. Maybe Phil was out roaming around in the middle of the night, and Walter came along and found out what he was doing. Phil could have killed him to cover up whatever it is and then tried to make his death look like a suicide."

Luke frowned as he thought it over. After a moment he said, "Yeah, that makes sense, I guess."

My thoughts were racing ahead. "They tried to act normal this morning, but instead of leaving early, Phil waited around with that story about his charter leaving later, but what he was really doing was waiting to see if the suicide story was going to hold up. When it didn't, he grabbed Sheila and took off."

Luke nodded again. "What could they be doing that's so bad Mr. Thompson had to kill Walter to keep it from being exposed?"

I spread my hands and shook my head. "That's a good question. I don't have an answer."

"I've been wondering where that shotgun came from, too."

"Maybe Phil had it with him. He could have wiped all his prints off of it after he shot Walter."

Luke's eyes widened. "Maybe he had the shotgun because he was planning to kill somebody else! Mr. Harvick could have interrupted him. So he postponed the other killing in hopes that the suicide story would fool everybody. He could use some other weapon later, instead of the shotgun."

Theories were flitting around in my head like butterflies in the resort's gardens. I said, "I didn't really think about it much until now, but Walter had to have been shot right there on the beach where he was found. You saw the . . . well, the mess it made on the sand."

Luke looked a little queasy again at the memory, but he nodded and said, "Yeah, that's right. Why would he have just stood there and let somebody put those shotgun barrels in his mouth?"

"Nobody would do that," I said. "He was either already dead or unconscious when it happened, which means he was attacked somewhere else and brought to the beach, where the killer tried to make it look like a Hemingway-inspired suicide."

Luke's eyes narrowed as he looked at me. "You know what you're doing, Miz D? You're bein' a detective again, and so am I!"

"No, we're not. We're just tryin' to figure out this mess . . ."

Well, maybe I was being a detective again, I realized. I couldn't help it. I'd been lied to and one of my clients had been killed. I like to think I'm pretty even-tempered, despite my red hair, but I was mad about the whole situation. The fact that similar things had happened before, on other tours, just made me angrier. And Luke was being dragged along for the ride.

Unfortunately, there was really nothing we could do to help find the killer, and I realized that, too. Detective Zimmer had already alerted the police to be on the lookout for Phil and Sheila Thompson, and I was sure he was checking into the ownership of the murder weapon and forensics techs were sifting through the rest of the evidence. If Phil – or Sheila, I supposed – hadn't killed Walter, then all the other most likely suspects were stuck here at the resort and sooner or later Zimmer would figure out who the guilty party was.

"We'll just let it go, Luke," I said. "That's all we can do. Detective Zimmer won't like it if we start tryin' to solve the case before he does. He might even arrest us for interferin' with his investigation."

"Maybe, but I'll still bet you could figure out who the killer is before he does."

"I appreciate that vote of confidence. I think we'd better butt out, though."

Despite what I said, it was hard to stop my brain from thinking along the lines of finding the killer. I wouldn't say that I was in the habit of solving crimes, but I'd done enough of it that my instincts went naturally in that direction.

To take my mind off of it, I stepped over to a big map of the Keys that hung on the wall of Tom's office and forced myself to concentrate on it. My eyes followed Highway One all the way down from Miami to Key West and then moved on over to the Dry Tortugas.

That was where Phil Thompson had said he was going fishing today. A lie, of course, or at least it sure appeared to be.

But maybe he was doing something else in the Dry Tortugas. There wasn't much over there except the Fort Jefferson National Monument. Some of the area was an ecological preserve, so fishing wasn't allowed there, but the fishing in the rest of the area was supposed to be very good. It was also a prime spot for sailing, swimming, and snorkeling. Charter boats and catamarans made the trip over there regularly. Back in the Thirties, Ernest Hemingway and his friends had gone over there pretty often on fishing expeditions.

Except for the three biggest islands in the chain, the smaller ones were always subject to tides and wind and storms. I had read that sometimes the smallest islands were actually swallowed up by the waters of the Gulf and the Atlantic and other islands formed in their place.

I couldn't see a thing about the Dry Tortugas that would prompt somebody to lie about what they were doing, let alone commit murder to keep it a secret.

While I was absent-mindedly peering at the map, Tom appeared in the office's open doorway and propped a shoulder against the jamb. "Is Charles through with the two of you?" he asked.

"Yeah," I told him.

"What was that all about, if you don't mind my asking?"

"I don't mind. I don't know if Detective Zimmer

would. I'll risk it, though. He was telling us that Phil and Sheila Thompson lied about Phil going deep-sea fishing."

Tom frowned. "Why would anybody lie about something like that?"

"That's what Luke and I were just tryin' to figure out. We didn't come up with any answers, though."

"Well, I thought you might like to know that I called Pete Nickleby to check on Ms. Scanlon. I called the hospital first, but they wouldn't tell me anything because I'm not a relative. Pete's her lawyer, so they had to talk to him." Tom sighed. "Of course, I had to stay on the phone with him and sort of talk him through it . . . The important thing is, after they pumped her stomach, Ms. Scanlon is conscious and stable. Still too groggy to talk very much, Pete said, but she should be all right."

Luke asked, "Did she say whether or not she intended to kill herself?

Tom shook his head. "I don't know. I didn't get into that with Pete. I was just making sure she was still alive and the prognosis looked fairly good."

"And I appreciate that," I told him. "It was very thoughtful of you, Tom."

He smiled and shrugged. "Just trying to help."

Luke asked, "So what do we do now?"

"Well, we can't leave," I said, "so what should you do when you're stuck at a luxurious beach resort?"

"Enjoy it?" Tom suggested.

"Exactly. We can't go down to the actual beach, but I was thinkin' about tryin' out that pool of yours."

"I think that sounds like an excellent idea," he said. "Meet you down there in fifteen minutes?"

I nodded. "I'll be there."

"I think I'll see if I can find somebody who'd like to play some tennis," Luke mused. "Might as well take advantage of it like you said, Mr. Bradenton."

With that settled, we went back to our rooms, Luke to put on something appropriate for playing tennis, me to change into the sleek, one-piece bathing suit I'd brought along. I knew I looked pretty good in it, if I do say so myself.

I had brought along a big sun hat, too. I pulled my hair back, settled the hat on my head, and tied a short, white terrycloth cover-up around my hips. A check in the mirror made me smile. Not bad for a middle-aged lady, I thought. I put on a pair of sunglasses, slipped my phone, wallet, room key, a bottle of sunscreen, and a towel into a colorful canvas beach bag, and headed for the pool.

It was late morning by now, and quite a few of the resort's guests were at the pool. They might be stuck here for the moment and angry about it, but they weren't going to let that stop them from having some fun. That was an admirable attitude.

Tom was stretched out on a lounge chair in the partial shade of some palms. Patches of light and shadow dappled his bronzed skin in a very appealing fashion. There was an empty chair next to him with a folded beach towel lying on it to keep anybody else from claiming it.

He was wearing sunglasses, but I could tell his eyes were following me anyway. "Very nice," he said as he reached over to pick up the beach towel and clear the lounge chair for me.

"Thanks," I said, meaning it for both the gesture and the compliment. I set my bag beside the chair, kicked off my sandals, and sat down. I wished my legs were a little more tan, but at least they weren't fish-belly white.

"I didn't know if you wanted to swim or just take it easy, but I grabbed a couple of these chairs anyway while they were empty."

"You did just the right thing," I told him. "It's been a long day, and it's not even noon yet!"

"I'm sorry things have worked out the way they have. Maybe you can still make the best out of some of the trip."

"I'm gonna try," I said as I closed my eyes and willed my muscles to loosen up and let go of some of the tension I was carrying around. "At least I'm not in the hospital and under suspicion of murder like Ronnie."

"Hush, now," Tom said softly. "Don't even think about that. Just relax."

I tried to follow his advice. I really did. With the heat to bask in, and the sounds of people enjoying themselves in the pool, and Tom's comforting presence close beside me, I should have been able to.

But I suddenly found myself unable to stop thinking about Walter Harvick's murder, mentally replaying that ugly scene on the beach, and as several facts abruptly snapped together in a way I hadn't seen them before, I found myself sitting up straight on the lounge chair.

"What is it?" Tom asked. He had propped himself up on an elbow and was frowning worriedly at me.

"Ronnie Scanlon didn't murder Walter," I said.

"I know you don't think she would have done that – "

"No, it's more than that," I broke in on him. "I *know* she didn't kill him. She couldn't have. And if Detective Zimmer will stop and think about it, he'll know she couldn't have, too."

Chapter 19

Tom took off his sunglasses and stared at me for a long moment. Finally he said, "I'm not following you."

"Luke and I were talking about this earlier," I said. "That shotgun blast happened on the beach. It had to, because of the way the blood and, uh, other things were scattered right there behind the body."

Tom nodded. "Yeah, that makes sense. It's kind of gross, but you're right."

"That would be what you expected if Walter committed suicide. But he didn't."

"We still just have Charles Zimmer's word for that," Tom pointed out. "We don't actually know why he's so convinced Mr. Harvick was murdered."

"No, we don't, but we sort of have to assume that he was, or else Detective Zimmer wouldn't have said so. He'd have just called it a suicide and closed the case."

"I suppose that's right. Go on."

"Luke pointed out that nobody would stand still for having a shotgun shoved in his mouth. At that point, you'd fight back, no matter what. Anybody would. But Walter couldn't, because he was either unconscious or already dead."

"So the killer attacked him somewhere else, then dragged him out there on the beach to set up the suicide scene," Tom said.

I shook my head. "No. That wouldn't work because it would leave drag marks in the sand."

"The killer could have brushed them out somehow."

"Maybe, but in the dark like that, he'd be running the risk of missing some of them and ruining his plan. It would be simpler and safer to pick Walter up, carry him out there, and then set him down and use the shotgun on him. That way there's no chance of drag marks and only one set of footprints leading out to where the body was found."

Tom thought about that some more. "What you're saying still makes sense," he admitted. "But if you're right, what about the footprints leading *away* from the body when the killer left?"

"He walked backwards," I said.

A smile spread slowly across Tom's face. "You're right," he said. "It had to have happened that way. But why couldn't Ronnie Scanlon have . . . Oh, I get it. You don't think she could have picked up Mr. Harvick and carried him out there like that."

"I don't guess it's absolutely impossible, but it's pretty darned unlikely," I said. "Walter wasn't the biggest guy in the world, but he wasn't a real lightweight, either. She would have had to put him over her shoulder and carry the shotgun, too. It didn't really register on me at the time, but I saw the tracks leading out to the body. They went pretty straight. I think Ronnie would have been weaving all over the place if she'd been carrying Walter."

"More than likely." He paused, then said, "It's not exactly what you'd call proof, Delilah. I'm sure Charles Zimmer wouldn't."

"Maybe not, but I'm convinced. I think Walter's killer had to be a man."

"Like Phil Thompson."

I nodded. "Exactly."

"Even though he doesn't have a motive."

"Walter could have stumbled onto whatever Phil was doing."

"That would have to be something pretty bad to make committing murder worthwhile."

"People have killed before to keep things from being exposed," I said.

Tom nodded. "I'm sure that's true. You've, ah, had more experience along those lines than I have. But if you're right, at least that means we don't have to worry about the killer striking again. The Thompsons are gone, and if they're guilty it's not likely they'll come back here. As a matter of fact, they had time to get off the island before anybody realized they weren't here anymore."

That depressing thought had occurred to me, too. Phil and Sheila could be back in Miami by now. They might even be on a plane, headed for who knows where.

Tom put his sunglasses back on and leaned his head against the chair. "Since we can't do anything," he continued, "I vote we get back to re-laxing."

"You're right," I said. I leaned back, too. I even closed my eyes, hoping that I might be lucky enough to doze off for a while.

Fat chance of that. My mind kept spinning,

insisting that I had seen or heard something in the past two days that might hold the key to Walter Harvick's murder.

Whatever it was – if it even existed – stubbornly eluded me.

But at least with my legs stretched out into the sun the way they were, I was able to work on my tan.

* * *

I actually did go to sleep, which surprised me. Not for long, though, because Tom woke me up to ask if I'd put on any sunscreen. He didn't want me to burn. I hadn't, so I got a plastic bottle of it from my beach bag and rubbed some on my legs.

"I'll do your shoulders and your back if you want," Tom volunteered.

"That sounds nice." I handed him the sun-screen. "Thanks."

The back of the lounge chair let down so that I could lie almost flat on my belly. That's what I did while Tom rubbed the sunscreen onto my shoulders and upper back. His hands were strong, and the touch of them felt good. I started to drift off into a haze of lassitude.

The sound of my cell phone's ringtone – "Margaritaville"; I'd changed it for this trip, cliché though it might be – made me curse the person who'd invented that bothersome gadget. I raised up onto an elbow and reached into my bag.

The display showed that Luke was calling. I didn't figure he would interrupt unless it was something important, so I thumbed the button to answer.

"What is it, Luke?"

"I thought you'd want to know, Miz D," he said. "The cops just showed up with Mr. and Mrs. Thompson."

That set me bolt upright on the chair. "Are you sure?" I asked him.

"Yeah, I was going back to the main house after playing a set of tennis with Matt Altman, and I saw a couple of uniformed officers leading them in. That Detective Zimmer was with them, too. I didn't get too close, but I know it was them."

I believed him. Luke wasn't the sort to make a mistake about something like that.

"All right," I told him as I slipped my feet back into my sandals. "Thanks for lettin' me know."

"What are you gonna do?"

"Well, Zimmer probably won't talk to me, but I'm going to try to find out what's going on anyway. They're still my clients, even if they are murder suspects."

If I could convince Zimmer that my theory about Ronnie Scanlon being unable to have murdered Walter was correct, then she wouldn't need a lawyer anymore. I wasn't sure I'd be doing Phil and Sheila any favors by siccing Pete Nickleby on them . . . but heck, if they'd killed Walter I wasn't sure I really wanted to do them any favors.

"I'll see you at the house," I added to Luke, then closed the phone as I stood up.

Tom was already on his feet. "What is it?"

"The police brought in Phil and Sheila Thompson. Luke saw them being taken into the main house."

That put a puzzled frown on Tom's face. "Why would they bring them here? If they're in custody, why weren't they taken to police headquarters?"

"No idea," I replied with a shake of my head. I

Livia J. Washburn

had said that a lot over the past few hours, but it was true. I really didn't have any idea.

And I didn't like that feeling.

I would have much rather stayed there letting Tom massage the knots out of my muscles under the guise of rubbing sunscreen on me, but I couldn't turn my back on clients, even potential murderers. If I knew the Thompsons were guilty it would be different, but I didn't know that yet.

I shrugged into that terrycloth cover-up. It was short enough to leave my legs mostly bare, which means it wasn't really the most appropriate costume for trying to worm some information out of the cops, but I didn't have much choice. I picked up my bag.

"I'll come with you," Tom said. "I want to know what's going on, too."

I couldn't blame him for that. Having all this happening at the resort that generations of his family had built up had to be bothering him, even though he didn't really show it.

We hurried along the path leading from the pool back to the main house. When we got there, Luke was waiting for us on the verandah, just outside the front doors, wearing the t-shirt and shorts he had worn to play tennis.

"They're upstairs," he greeted us. "I watched through the window while Detective Zimmer and the other officers took them up there. They cleared everybody out, and there's a cop posted at the foot of the stairs now to keep anybody else from going up."

"We'll see about that," Tom said. "This is my place, after all, and I'm starting to think Charles is taking advantage of our friendship."

We went into the lobby and crossed the room to

the stairs. The officer posted there held up a hand to stop us.

"Nobody allowed upstairs now, sir," he told Tom. "Sorry."

"You know I own this resort, don't you?"

"Yes, but that doesn't matter. You'll have to take it up with Detective Zimmer."

"I plan to," Tom said, and I couldn't help but notice that an angry note had come into his voice.

I asked the officer, "How long do you expect them to be up there?"

He shook his head. "I couldn't tell you, ma'am."

"Where were the Thompsons taken into custody?"

"I couldn't – "

"Never mind," I said. "I know, you couldn't tell me."

He shrugged as if to say that wasn't his fault. And I knew it wasn't. That didn't make the situation any less frustrating.

Other people were in the lobby, too, looking just as curious as we were. Unlike the three of us, though, they hung back from the foot of the stairs, content just to watch and see what happened next. They didn't have any real stake in this.

"Were Phil and Sheila handcuffed when you saw them?" I asked Luke.

He shook his head. "No, but they didn't look like they were going anywhere except where the cops wanted them to."

The front doors opened again, and two more officers came in with a prisoner between them and another officer bringing up the rear, as if the guy they had in custody was dangerous.

I didn't doubt that was the case, because all it took for me to recognize him was a glance. I had seen him in Sloppy Joe's the night before. So much had happened since then it seemed hard to believe that not much more than twelve hours had passed.

The dark, hawkish face of Clint Drake was set in angry lines. Unlike the Thompsons, he was handcuffed. Or rather, he had some of those plastic restraints around his wrists, pinning them behind his back as one of the cops held his arm and steered him across the lobby toward the stairs. A streak of dried blood from a cut on Drake's forehead was smeared across his face.

"What in the world?" I muttered.

"Who's that?" Luke asked as the little group advanced toward us. He hadn't been at Sloppy Joe's the night before, so he'd never seen Drake.

"Step back," the cop on duty at the foot of the stairs ordered us.

As we moved aside to let them pass, Tom said quietly to Luke, "That's Clint Drake. One of our local shady characters."

"Walter was trying to charter his boat," I added.

"Ohhh-kay," Luke said, clearly confused.

He was no different in that respect than I was.

Drake glared at us as he was escorted past us and started up the stairs with the officers. I don't know if he recognized me or if he was just mad at the world in general because he'd been arrested.

A familiar rumbling voice made me look up. Detective Zimmer had appeared on the second floor landing. "Officer Bell," he called down to the cop who had stopped us, "I want those three up here right now."

And then he pointed at me, Tom, and Luke.

Chapter 20

A shiver of apprehension went through me. I don't know why; I was sure I hadn't done anything wrong except maybe acting a little more curious about Walter Harvick's murder than Detective Zimmer would have preferred. I guess it's like driving and suddenly seeing a police car in your rearview mirror. Even though you know you haven't been speeding or breaking any other traffic laws, you still feel a little nervous.

In this case, it was more like a lot nervous. Zimmer had that effect on people, I supposed, especially when he didn't look happy.

I wondered how long it had been since Detective Zimmer actually had looked happy.

Then I shook off that thought as the uniformed cop said, "You heard the detective. You can go upstairs now."

"I'm not sure I want to anymore," I said.

"Ms. Dickinson," Zimmer said.

Tom touched my arm. He looked eager to find out what was going on as he said, "Come on, let's get up there before he changes his mind."

He had a point there. With Tom and Luke flanking me, I started up the stairs.

Zimmer met us at the top. He jerked his head to indicate that we should follow him.

As we turned to the right, I saw that the door to the Thompsons' room was open, with a policeman standing just outside it. I figured that meant the other cops, as well as Phil and Sheila, and Clint Drake, were inside the room. When we reached the door, I saw that I was right. Phil and Sheila sat next to each other on the bed, looking scared, while Clint Drake, still in his restraints, stood to one side of the room with an officer on either side of him.

As soon as he saw me, Phil exclaimed, "Ms. Dickinson! Thank God. Will you tell these officers Sheila and I aren't some sort of criminals?"

He looked and sounded so pathetic, for a second I felt sorry for him. Then I remembered how Walter Harvick's body had looked, sprawled there on the sand. Until I knew for sure that Phil and Sheila hadn't had anything to do with that, I wasn't going to waste any pity on them.

"I don't see how I can do that, Mr. Thompson," I said coolly. "All I know is what you've told me, and it seems like you've got a habit of lyin'."

"The only thing I lied about was that I was going fishing," Phil said. "I . . . I had something else I wanted to do."

Detective Zimmer grunted and said disgustedly, "Treasure hunting."

"It's more like amateur archeology in a way – "

"Treasure hunting!" Zimmer repeated, clearly not pleased. He waved a hand at the maps and charts spread out on the bed and the books stacked on the room's desk.

"Really?" Tom said with a note of amusement in

his voice. "You came down here to look for buried treasure?"

Phil looked pained. "There are still plenty of legendary treasures to be found – "

"They're legendary because they're not really there," Tom told him. "There have been a lot more rumors about buried treasure than there ever was any real treasure."

"You don't know that," Phil insisted. "Anything might be buried on these little islands. I've been studying the subject for years, and this isn't the first time I've come down here to search."

"But you haven't found anything, have you?"

Phil didn't answer Tom's question right away. He sat there scowling for several seconds before he slowly shook his head.

"Not yet. But it's just a matter of time."

Zimmer looked at me and asked, "Did you know anything about this?"

"Not a thing," I said. "Don't you think I'd have told you if I did?"

"I hope so."

I nodded toward Clint Drake and asked, "What's his part in this? Was it his boat Mr. Thompson was on yesterday?"

Phil didn't let Zimmer answer. He said, "That's right. I chartered his boat to help in the search. And then today he tried to kidnap us!"

Drake spoke for the first time since we'd been up here, rasping, "You misunderstood."

"You said you wouldn't bring us back to Key West unless I called my bank and had fifty thousand dollars wired to your offshore account!" Phil said. "And the things you threatened to do to my wife . . ."

Beside him on the bed, Sheila shuddered.

"If all this is true," Zimmer said, "the two of you are lucky. Drake might have done even worse. He would have cut your throats and dropped you over the side for the sharks if he'd gotten what he wanted from you first."

"That's a damned lie," Drake said.

Zimmer ignored him and went on, "You said you had things here in your room that would verify your story, Thompson. If you mean these maps and books, that doesn't really help you. Even if you came down here to search for buried treasure – " The disdainful way Zimmer said it made it clear he felt the same way about the subject that Tom did. " – that doesn't mean you didn't kill Walter Harvick."

"We didn't even know that man," Sheila said. "We said hello to him, that's all."

"Then why did the two of you sneak off as soon as you heard he'd been killed?" Zimmer demanded.

"One thing didn't have anything with the other," Phil insisted. "I just didn't want to lose a day of searching. Today might have been the day when I finally found what I've been looking for . . . the gold of San Cristobal."

Tom winced. "That's just a legend, and not even a very good one."

"No, it's real," Phil said with the zealotry of the true believer. "The Spanish galleon *San Cristobal* went down somewhere here in the Keys, but the captain and some of the crew were able to salvage a chest of gold they were taking back to Spain and take it with them in a small boat. They buried it on the first island they came to, planning to come back and retrieve it later, after they were rescued. But they set out again in the boat because there was no food or fresh water on that island, and all of them died except for one crewman, and he was half insane from thirst and the sun when he was found by another ship. He was never able to lead anybody back to the island where they hid the gold."

"It's a fairy tale," Tom said.

"No, it's not." Phil stood up. Zimmer tensed, but Phil pointed to the books on the desk and went on, "I can show you. I found records of the old documents that contain the story. The crewman who survived remembered enough clues that I was able to put them together and use maps from the Sixteenth Century to narrow down the area where the treasure might have been hidden. Sheila and I, we've kept all that secret, but . . . but I suppose we can share it if it means we won't be blamed for killing that man. Anyway, when we left here this morning, we thought he had committed suicide. Nothing had been said about a murder."

"We just wanted to find the treasure and be able to retire," Sheila said wistfully. "To finally get away from all those horrible kids . . ."

Phil was still edging toward the desk and the stacks of research books. Zimmer put out a hand and said, "Forget about the treasure. Where were the two of you last night?"

"Right here," Phil answered without hesitation. "We worked on the maps and then went to sleep."

"But no one can confirm that."

"Well . . . no, I suppose not. We were together, so we, uh, alibi each other, I guess."

Zimmer's snort made it clear how much he thought of that alibi.

"Last chance," he said. "Convince me that you didn't have anything to do with Harvick's death, or I'm placing you under arrest."

"Just because we snuck out today?" Sheila said. "That's the only evidence you have against us?"

"Flight can be presumed to be evidence of guilt."

"We weren't fleeing," Phil said. "We would have come back on our own." He glared at Drake. "That is, if we hadn't been double-crossed."

Drake just sneered and looked away.

While I wasn't quite ready to admit that I didn't think the Thompsons were responsible for Walter's murder, I was leaning toward believing their story. They both certainly sounded sincere. And Sheila was right: Zimmer didn't really have a case against them. There wasn't a shred of motive, and no physical evidence to link them to the case, as far as I knew. Of course, the police could have turned up a lot of things I didn't know about.

Were the two of them fanatical enough in their belief in the treasure they were hunting to regard Walter as a threat if he found out what they were doing? It was possible, I supposed, but I had trouble believing it. Again, making that case would require being able to prove that Phil had been outside the main house last night.

Zimmer sighed. "We're going to need to take your statements about what happened today with Drake anyway. The officers will escort you to the police department and somebody there will talk to you."

"We're not under arrest?" Phil said.

"Not yet." Zimmer didn't bother trying to hide his disappointment as he said that.

Drake spoke up. "I'm telling you again, this is all a misunderstanding."

"We'll see," Zimmer said. "Get him out of here."

The officers took Drake out of the room. Phil and Sheila went along, too, leaving Zimmer there with me, Tom, and Luke.

"This room is off-limits until we've conducted a

thorough search of it," Zimmer told Tom.

"That's fine." Tom smiled faintly. "With everything else that's been going on, what's a little more crime scene tape?"

"I appreciate you being so understanding about it, Tom."

I said, "If you don't mind me asking, Detective, what happened out on Drake's boat? Did he really try to kidnap the Thompsons?"

"I wouldn't put it past him," Zimmer said. "We've suspected that he's dumped more than one body over the side in the past, but we've never been able to prove it. There might have been two more today if Mrs. Thompson hadn't called for help. Drake probably didn't count on her having a satellite phone or the guts to use it after he threatened them. A Coast Guard cutter happened to be close by . . ." Zimmer shrugged. "I think they were really lucky. That luck was the real treasure they found today."

"Do you think they killed Mr. Harvick?" Tom asked.

Zimmer was more talkative than I had seen him so far, maybe because he was getting frustrated with the case. He said, "There's no real reason to think so, if we accept their story about looking for buried treasure." He swung his big hand toward the maps and books. "If it's a lie, they went to an awful lot of trouble to prepare, and that doesn't jibe with the fact that they didn't know Walter Harvick before this tour. We haven't been able to turn up any connection between them and him. If Thompson killed Harvick, it must have been a spur of the moment thing."

"It sounds pretty unlikely to me, Detective," I said.

He looked at me. "And you're speaking with the voice of experience, aren't you, Ms. Dickinson? I spared a few minutes earlier to look you up on the Internet. You've made a habit of solving murders."

It was my turn to shrug. "I was trying to get things settled down so my tours could continue."

"It doesn't look like you're going to be able to salvage much of this one, unless you've got the solution hidden up your sleeve."

I shook my head and said, "Afraid not."

Tom asked, "So are you back to considering Ms. Scanlon your primary suspect? Because if you are, Delilah has some more thoughts on that."

"Really?" Zimmer raised his eyebrows. "I'd like to hear them."

I hesitated. Tom said, "Go ahead, Delilah. What you told me makes sense."

With that urging, I laid out my theory about how Walter had been killed somewhere else and then carried out onto the beach to set up the apparent suicide, which meant it was nearly impossible for Ronnie to have done it. Zimmer appeared to be paying close attention as he listened.

When I was finished, he nodded and said, "The same thoughts crossed my mind, Ms. Dickinson. I don't mind admitting that. You seem to think like a homicide detective."

"I don't know about that. I just don't think there's much of a case against Ronnie."

He surprised me by saying, "I'm inclined to agree with you. One of our officers was able to get a statement from Ms. Scanlon a little while ago, and she admitted that she took sleeping pills in an attempt to end her life." He sighed. "It appears that we're back where we started."

Since he wasn't being quite so stiff-necked right

now, I took a chance on asking another question. "Are you still sure Walter's death was murder and not a successful suicide?"

"Positive," Zimmer said. "The ME found a bone fragment from the skull lodged in the back of Harvick's throat."

"Not to be too crude about it," Tom said, "but I'd think a double load of buckshot would produce a lot of bone fragments."

"But not in the throat," Zimmer said. "The shotgun blast was angled up. All the fragments would have been blown upward and out the back of what used to be Harvick's head. The doctor thinks it's more likely this fragment came from an earlier shot, probably from a handgun, that entered Harvick's forehead angling down." Zimmer's face took on a grim cast. "Whoever killed him put him on his knees first, maybe even forced him to beg for his life. And then the son of a bitch pulled the trigger anyway."

Chapter 21

I knew that grim image was going to linger in my mind. I tried to force it away and said, "So the shotgun blast was intended to cover up the evidence of the earlier shot, as well as make Walter's death look like suicide."

Zimmer nodded. "That's the way it looks to me, and the ME agrees. It would have worked if he hadn't spotted that bone fragment. The case would be closed now, ruled a suicide."

"Bad luck for the killer," Tom said, "but good luck for you."

Zimmer grunted. "I should let you people go on about your business," he said.

"That's hard to do when we're stuck here," I pointed out. "We were supposed to take the trolley tour of Old Town today."

"Sorry," Zimmer muttered, but I wasn't sure he really was. His only real concern was catching a killer, and I couldn't blame him for that.

A couple of the uniformed cops came back, and Zimmer started to usher us out, saying that he and the other officers were going to search the room.

"I probably shouldn't say this, but do you have a warrant for that?" Tom asked.

"Don't need one," Zimmer said. "The Thompsons gave us permission."

"But they don't own the place. I do."

"Since they're renting the room, legally they can grant permission to conduct a search."

Tom frowned. "Is that right?"

"Well, it would probably look better to a judge if you granted permission, too . . ."

Tom waved a hand and said, "Go ahead. If Mr. and Mrs. Thompson don't care, I suppose neither do I."

"Thanks," Zimmer said with a nod. He motioned for the uniformed officers to get at it.

Tom, Luke, and I went back downstairs. I was still dressed for the pool, but my stomach reminded me that it was time for lunch and I hadn't had anything but coffee for breakfast. At the time, so soon after seeing Walter's body on the beach, I had felt like I'd never have an appetite again. The hours that had passed since then had changed my mind. An empty belly is an insistent thing.

"I probably should have changed clothes so we could get something to eat," I commented as we passed the dining room entrance.

"A bathing suit's no reason not to get some lunch," Tom said. "People do it all the time. Besides, you look great."

I shook my head. "I wouldn't feel comfortable sitting in there like this."

"How about eating out on the patio, then?" he suggested. "I'll tell the staff to send out some sandwiches and drinks for us."

"Now that sounds good," I admitted. "I didn't know you had a patio dining area like that."

"It's a well-kept secret," Tom said with a smile. He pointed to a door. "Go down that hall and a-round the corner, and you'll see another door lead-ing outside."

"Okay. You coming, Luke?"

"Yeah, I guess," Luke said. "If I won't be intruding."

"Not at all," Tom told him. "You two go ahead. I'll join you in a few minutes."

We followed Tom's directions and found our-selves on a small, brick patio that held four wrought-iron and glass tables with four chairs at each one. Shrubs surrounded it, giving it a semblance of privacy. Over the years, the main house had been added onto numerous times in a haphazard fashion, which meant it sprawled around and created little out of the way corners like this one. We were the only people out here.

After we sat down, Luke asked, "What will we do if Detective Zimmer hasn't found the murderer by the time we're supposed to leave to go back to Miami? Do you think he'll let us leave?"

"I don't think he'll have any choice," I said. "By then everybody who was here when Walter was killed will have been questioned, and once he has those statements he won't be able to hold anybody who hasn't been charged with a crime."

"Then the killer will get away with it," Luke muttered.

"Not necessarily. Zimmer could still come up with some evidence and have a suspect brought back here. Besides, it's possible the killer actually lives here in Key West."

Luke frowned. "You think so?"

"Tom's got, what, a dozen or more people on his staff? They're all bound to know their way around this place. We've been focused on the tourists, but I'll bet Detective Zimmer is looking into the staff, too. Maybe one of them was up to something illegal and Walter found out about it."

"Yeah," Luke said, growing more interested. "That sounds possible. But we don't have any way of investigating them."

"That's why the police will have to do it," I said. "That's their job to start with."

"Sure, but I haven't given up yet on you solving this case, Miz D."

"You might as well," I told him. "I think I'm out of my depth on this one."

"I'll believe that when I see it."

Tom emerged from the house. He had gotten a Bradenton Beach Resort t-shirt from somewhere and pulled it on, so I guess he looked a little more respectable, if not quite as breathtakingly attracttive. "Our lunch will be here in a few minutes," he announced as he sat down at the table with Luke and me.

"Thanks," I said.

Luke said, "We were just talking about – "

That was as far as he got before I kicked his ankle.

Unfortunately, he said, "Ow!" and jerked his leg.

"Sorry," I murmured. "Didn't mean to do that."

I knew he'd been about to tell Tom we'd been discussing the possibility that one of the people who worked for him might have killed Walter. I figured that might offend him, and I didn't want to do that.

I went on, "We were talkin' about how Detective Zimmer's gonna have to let us go back to Miami when our time here is up. He'll have statements from everybody by then, and I'm sure you have other guests comin' in who'll need our rooms."

"Well, I haven't had anybody cancel their reservations yet," Tom said with a smile. "But maybe the word hasn't gotten around about the murder. It'll be a big story here in Key West, but probably not anywhere else."

"I'm sorry if the case damages the reputation of the resort."

"You don't have anything to apologize for, Delilah," he said. "Like I told you, Key West was founded by shady characters. Great-grandfather Claude wasn't exactly a paragon of virtue. The family had fallen on hard times during the Twenties, and there were rumors that he kept things going by running rum from Cuba. Of course, once he turned this place into a resort and it became popular, he was a respectable businessman, so nobody ever mentioned the rum-running again."

"Yeah, but rum-running is glamorous," Luke said. "Murder isn't."

Tom shrugged. "That's true. But we'll weather the storm. We've weathered plenty of actual storms, and a little bad publicity is nothing compared to a hurricane."

A couple of the teenage girls who worked in the dining room brought out trays that held sandwiches, potato chips, and tall glasses of iced tea that started to sweat as soon as they hit the outside air. The three of us dug in. Turkey and avocado sandwiches might not be gourmet fare, but they tasted pretty good just then, especially washed down with iced tea.

We had just about finished eating when the door into the house opened and Matt and Aimee Altman came out onto the patio, holding hands. They weren't looking for a secluded place to eat lunch, though. They seemed nervous.

"Ms. Dickinson," Matt began. "We were looking for you, and one of the girls in the dining room said you were out here . . ."

"It's all right, Matt," I said. I had a hard time calling somebody as young as him "Mr. Altman". He and Aimee both looked like they could almost still be in high school, although I knew they were older than that. "What can I do for you?"

"People have been saying that, well, you're sort of a detective."

Blasted smart-phones. Anybody can Google anything, anywhere, these days.

"Not really," I said in response to Matt's comment.

"But you've been mixed up in murders before and actually solved them."

I shrugged.

"We know you've been talking to that Detective Zimmer a lot," Aimee put in. "Are the two of you working together on the case?"

"Not exactly," I said, although in our last conversation Zimmer had shared more information and more of his thoughts than I'd ever expected him to.

Matt started to say something else, but he stopped and looked first at Luke and then at Tom, as if their presence was holding him back somehow.

"If there's something you want to tell me," I said, "don't worry about Luke and Mr. Bradenton. They know as much about the case as I do."

I didn't see how either of the Altmans could know anything useful about Walter's murder, but I recalled that Walter and Matt had had that little skirmish at the Hemingway House the day before.

Zimmer knew about that, and it had to have put Matt on his radar, at least a little. Maybe Matt was scared that he would wind up being blamed for the murder.

I just couldn't see Matt Altman putting a gun to Walter's head and pulling the trigger, much less hauling the body out onto the beach and setting up that apparent suicide. Maybe I was naïve, but I didn't think either of them was that diabolical.

That's what Matt was worried about, though. With Aimee urging him on, he asked, "Has Detective Zimmer said anything to you about considering me a suspect?"

"Should he?" I asked in return, not answering Matt's question just yet.

He looked a little sick. "Of course not. I . . . I didn't hurt anybody."

"Matt would never kill anybody," Aimee put in. "It's just that since he was the last one to see Mr. Harvick last night – "

"Wait a minute," I broke in. "What did you say?"

Chapter 22

Tom and Luke sat up straighter, too. Matt groaned and said, "Aimee, you shouldn't have just blurted it out like that. I was getting around to it."

"I'm sorry," she said as she clutched his arm. "I just don't want you to be arrested!"

"You won't be arrested if you haven't done anything wrong," I told Matt . . . even though I knew that wasn't always the case. Innocent men had found themselves behind bars before.

"I . . . I just don't know what to do," Matt went on. "I . . . lied to the cops when they questioned us about where we were last night."

"I lied, too," Aimee said. "I should go to jail, too."

"Nobody's goin' to jail yet," I said. "Just settle down and tell me what you're talkin' about."

Matt took a deep breath. "We told the officer who talked to us that we were in our cottage all night. The guy . . . well, he sort of looked at Aimee, and I could tell that he believed us."

Aimee gave us a weak smile.

"But actually I got out and took a walk in the middle of the night," Matt said.

"We sort of had a fight," Aimee added. "It didn't really amount to anything."

"And it was all my fault," Matt said as he turned to look at her.

"No, it was all my fault," she insisted.

I didn't want to sit there listening to them arguing about whose fault the argument was, each eager to take all the blame on themselves like young married couples do. I said, "Just go on with the story, Matt."

"Okay. I went for a walk, you know, to cool off a little, and I ran into Mr. Harvick over by the stable."

"What time was this?" I asked.

"I'm not sure. Sometime between two and three o'clock in the morning, I'd say."

I nodded. That gave Walter and Ronnie time to get back to the resort from Captain Tony's, do whatever carrying on they'd done in Walter's room, and then go to sleep. Ronnie had gone to sleep, anyway, a deep slumber fueled by booze and the afterglow of lovemaking. Walter, obviously, hadn't been quite that tired.

"What happened when the two of you ran into each other?"

"There wasn't a fight," Matt said quickly. "I swear, there wasn't any trouble at all."

"It's true," Aimee put in. "There wasn't a mark on Matt when he came back, not a single scratch or bruise."

He turned to her, an expression of slightly wounded pride on his face, and said, "Well, even if there had been a fight, I probably wouldn't have had a mark on me. We're talking about Walter Harvick here."

I remembered how Walter had handled Rollie Cranston with ease in Sloppy Joe's and wasn't so sure Matt's confidence was justified. But there was no point in bringing that up, so I said, "Go on, Matt. What happened?"

"Nothing, really. I said hello and he asked me what I was doing out there at that time of night. I told him I was just taking a walk."

"Did he tell you what he was doing?" Tom asked.

Matt shook his head. "No, and I didn't think to ask him. I was upset about that fight with Aimee – "

"You couldn't even hardly call it a fight," she said. "It was more of a spat."

"Yeah, that's true. Anyway, I was so distracted that I just told Mr. Harvick to have a good night and turned around to go back to the cottage. By then I was over being mad and just wanted to go back and apologize and . . . and make up with Aimee."

The way she blushed told me they'd made up real good.

"And that's it," Matt went on. "So you see, it didn't really amount to anything. But I did talk to Mr. Harvick, so I know he was still alive then and I know where he was, but I didn't tell the cops about it because I was afraid they'd jump to the conclusion I had something to do with his death because of the trouble he and I had with each other at the Hemingway House yesterday."

By the time he was finished the words were rushing out of his mouth in a nervous jumble. I understood why he was worried, and I understood why he hadn't told everything to the cops, too. They're trained to look for the simplest answer, because to be fair, the simplest answer is usually the right one. They knew about the trouble between Walter and Matt because I'd told Detective Zimmer about it. If they knew that Matt and Walter had been together in the middle of the night, not long before Walter was killed, sure they would consider Matt a strong suspect. There was no doubt in my mind about that.

But I didn't doubt Matt's innocence, either. If he had killed Walter, he wouldn't have been so worried about lying to the police that he would come to me and spill his guts like this. He would have just kept his mouth shut, hoping to ride out the investigation and get away with his crime.

Would Detective Zimmer see it that way, though? I couldn't answer that question.

Matt asked me an even harder one. He said, "What do you think I should do, Ms. Dickinson?"

I took a deep breath to give me a couple more seconds to think about it. Then I said, "You're gonna have to talk to the police again, Matt. It'll be better for you if you tell them what you did instead of letting them find out for themselves."

"But he can't do that!" Aimee protested as she clutched his arm. "They'll put him in jail!"

"Not necessarily. They might charge him with obstruction of justice or concealing evidence or something like that, but if the information about where Walter was helps them find the killer, they probably won't press charges."

"But what if they decide he killed Mr. Harvick, no matter what he says?"

Matt muttered, "I'm still right here, you know."

I looked at him and said, "Matt, did you kill Walter Harvick?"

"Absolutely not!" The answer came back quick and steady. "I'd never do anything like that."

"You'll have to convince the police the same way you convinced me."

He nodded glumly. "I can do that. I hope."

Aimee said, "There's one thing you can do to help him, Ms. Dickinson. Find the real killer. Then everybody will know that Matt's not guilty."

I shook my head. "I told you, honey, I'm not really a detective – "

"But you solved those other crimes! I know you can solve this one, too."

Matt said, "Aimee, that's not fair – "

"I don't care about fair!" she burst out. "I just don't want my husband locked up in prison!"

I couldn't argue with that sentiment. Aimee looked so scared and miserable that without thinking about what I was saying, I told her, "All right, I'll see what I can find out."

"You will?" she gave me a shaky smile, then stepped forward and leaned over to give me a spon- -taneous hug. "Thank you, Ms. Dickinson. I'm sure you'll find out who really killed poor Mr. Harvick."

Matt said, "I don't know that I'd call him poor Mr. Harvick. Just because he's dead now doesn't mean he was any less of a jerk when he was alive."

"I don't think I'd let the cops hear me say anything like that, if I was you," Tom advised him dryly.

"You're right, I won't." He turned to me and went on, "Thanks, Ms. Dickinson. I appreciate anything you can do to help me. You still think I ought to go to the police and tell them what I know?"

"I do," I said with a nod. "In fact, if Detective Zimmer is still around, I'll go with you to talk to him. Just let me go upstairs and put on some clothes first."

Tom said, "We're not going back to the pool?" He sounded a little disappointed, which sort of pleased me.

"I'm afraid not. But I'll take a rain check."

"I'll hold you to that," he said.

That sounded good, especially the part about him holding me.

* * *

The conversation with Matt and Aimee Altman hadn't really changed anything about what I was doing, I thought as I got into a pair of Capri pants and a blouse. Even though I'd denied it, even to myself, I'd been trying to figure out what had happened to Walter Harvick ever since I'd seen his body lying on the beach. Even when his death appeared to be suicide, I'd been trying to figure out why he would have killed himself.

So the fact that I'd promised Aimee Altman I'd investigate . . . well, I was already doing just that, wasn't I?

Maybe I wouldn't say anything about it to Detective Zimmer, though. No point in throwing it in his face.

I'd told Matt I would meet him and Aimee in the lobby. When I got down there, they were waiting, looking nervous. I didn't blame them for that. I thought we could make Zimmer listen to reason, but there was no guarantee of that.

Luke was there with them, keeping an eye on them. I had asked him, discreetly, to do that so they wouldn't panic and do something crazy like try to get away from the resort, the way Phil and Sheila Thompson had. He gave me an unobtrusive nod to let me know that there hadn't been any trouble. I didn't see Tom anywhere, but the door of his office was closed so I thought he might be in there.

Despite the murder, there was still work to be done in order to keep the resort running smoothly.

"All right, you two," I told the Altmans. "Are you ready to do this?"

"No," Matt said, "but I don't think I'll ever be ready, so we might as well go ahead and get it over with."

They went up the stairs hand in hand, clinging to each other for support. That was sweet. It wouldn't last, I thought with the inevitable disillusionment of middle age, but for right now it was sweet indeed and I sort of envied them.

An officer was still standing outside the door of the Thompsons' room. When we came up to him, I asked, "Is Detective Zimmer inside?"

"Just a minute," he said. He opened the door and disappeared inside the room. A moment later Zimmer's burly form filled the doorway.

"What is it, Ms. Dickinson?" he asked. His gaze flicked past me to Matt and Aimee and his eyes narrowed slightly.

"The Altmans and I need to talk to you, Detective," I said. "It has to do with the case."

"I've already glanced at their statement," Zimmer said. "Seemed pretty straightforward."

Matt said, "I lied, Detective."

I wished he hadn't phrased it quite so bluntly, but there it was and the words couldn't be called back now. Zimmer's eyes narrowed even more, and he said, "We've just about wrapped up the search of this room, so maybe we'd better go somewhere else and talk about this."

"Did you find anything?" I asked, not really expecting him to answer me.

He didn't. He just said, "Come on. We'll go down to Mr. Bradenton's office."

With that tone of voice and the glare on his face, there was no arguing with him. We went.

Chapter 23

A few minutes earlier I had thought that Tom might be in his office, but he wasn't. It was empty, we found when Detective Zimmer knocked on the door and then opened it when he didn't get any response. Tom had given him permission to use it, though, so he waved us in and followed behind us, closing the door firmly.

"Now what's all this about lying to the police?" he asked as he went around the desk.

"I didn't really mean to," Matt said. "I just got scared."

"Matt would never do anything wrong," Aimee said. "He's very honest and law-abiding. He doesn't speed or talk on his cell phone in school zones or anything."

"Murder's a little more serious than that," Zimmer said.

Matt nodded. "I know. That's why I decided I had to tell you what happened."

Zimmer folded his arms across his chest, scowled, and said, "Go ahead."

Matt swallowed hard, then launched into the

story. Zimmer listened expressionlessly. Matt finally said, "That's all there was to it, Detective. I went back to our cottage and didn't see Mr. Harvick after that. I still haven't . . . and if the rumors I've heard about what happened to him are right, I'm glad I haven't."

"You and Walter Harvick had a fight yesterday," Zimmer rumbled.

"It wasn't really a fight," Aimee said. "Just some harsh words, that's all."

Zimmer ignored her and continued staring at Matt. "Then you had a fight with your wife last night. Sounds to me like you're a pretty hot-tempered guy, Mr. Altman."

"He's not," Aimee said. "Not at all. He's the sweetest, gentlest man on earth."

"You sure about that, ma'am?"

Aimee drew herself up straighter. She looked like she didn't appreciate having her words challenged like that.

"Of course I'm sure," she snapped. "I'm married to him, aren't I? I ought to know better than anyone what he's like."

"There have been plenty of marriages that have proven that theory wrong."

I couldn't help but agree with Zimmer about that. My own divorce had been fairly amicable, but things had come out during the course of it that I hadn't known about my ex-husband, and I was sure he felt the same way about me.

Zimmer turned his attention back to Matt. "You said you ran into Harvick near the stable. What was he doing?"

"I don't know. Just walking along. He may have been out for a stroll, too."

That was possible. If Walter hadn't been able to

sleep, he might have slipped out for some exercise, rather than tossing and turning and disturbing Ronnie.

That didn't really seem likely to me, though. As tightly wound as Walter had appeared to be during the short time I knew him, he struck me as the sort who always had a reason for what he was doing, no matter what it was. He wouldn't be walking aimlessly.

"And what did he do after the two of you exchanged greetings?"

"I told you, I turned around and went back to the cottage. I don't have any idea what he did. The area isn't very well lit at night. Anyway, I didn't look back. I was anxious to get back to Aimee."

"Ready to kiss and make up, eh?" Zimmer shook his head and raised a hand. "Sorry, that was unprofessional of me. Why didn't you tell the truth about all this when the officer questioned you?"

"Because I knew you'd probably heard about the little fracas as the Hemingway House. I was afraid I'd get blamed for Mr. Harvick's death."

Aimee said, "You can see why he'd feel that way, can't you, Detective?"

Zimmer ignored her. He glared at Matt and asked, "Is there anything else you want to tell me, Mr. Altman?"

Matt took a deep breath and shook his head. "No, that's it. I've told you everything that happened . . . and I have to admit, it feels good to get it off my chest."

I said to Zimmer, "You won't be able to use any of that, you know. You didn't give him any sort of Miranda warning and he didn't have a lawyer present."

"This wasn't an official interrogation," Zimmer

said. "I'm still just trying to find out what happened."

"I hope this helps," Matt said. "At least now you know that Mr. Harvick was still alive between two and three o'clock, and that he was over by the stable."

Zimmer grunted dismissively, as if to say that he didn't know if that would help or not. He said to Matt and Aimee, "The two of you can go. Just don't leave the resort, like before."

"Thank you, Detective," Aimee said. "I'm so glad you believe Matt – "

"Come on, Aimee," Matt said, taking her arm to steer her out of the office before she could gush any more.

I started to follow them, but Zimmer said, "Not you, Ms. Dickinson."

I stopped and looked back at him, surprised that he wasn't letting me go, too. "What is it, Detective?"

"Close the door."

I closed the door behind Matt and Aimee. Zimmer sank into the chair behind the desk and motioned for me to sit down, too. When I had, he said, "What do you think of young Altman's story?"

"You're askin' my opinion?"

"That sheriff's department investigator from Georgia you mentioned, Timothy Farrady, called me back a little while ago. He said you'd be liable to drive me absolutely crazy, but that you were pretty smart and had good instincts. Farraday seemed to know what he was talking about, so I'll ask you again . . . do you believe Altman?"

"Yeah, I do," I replied without hesitation. "Before all this happened, he was a little cocky and arrogant, but he seemed like a basically decent kid.

They both do."

"So young."

"Yes, they are."

"Bonnie and Clyde were young," Zimmer mused.

"Matt and Aimee Altman are no Bonnie and Clyde."

He actually smiled at that. "No, they're not. It looks bad, him lying like he did the first time around, but I guess it's understandable."

A thought had occurred to me, so I said, "You know, Matt's not the only one who had trouble with Walter at the Hemingway House."

"You're talking about Rollie Cranston."

"That's right." I hated to throw suspicion on Rollie, who had seemed to be a fairly likable sort of guy, if not my type. But I could see him killing Walter a lot easier than I could see Matt Altman in that role.

"And Cranston had a run-in with Harvick at Sloppy Joe's the night before last, too," Zimmer went on.

"He sure did. Walter put him on his knees." I thought about what Zimmer had said earlier about the killer making Walter beg for his life. "Maybe Rollie decided to return the favor."

"That's a good theory. Unfortunately, after you left him last night, Cranston picked up a 35-year-old librarian from Illinois and spent the night with her at the Hyatt. She was pretty adamant that Cranston was in bed with her during the window of time in which Harvick was killed, and there are witnesses among the hotel staff who saw him there before and after that, too."

Somehow I wasn't surprised. Rollie probably had plenty of success picking up female tourists with his Hemingway lookalike bit. His alibi sounded unshakable.

"Then if we rule out Rollie Cranston, and we believe Matt Altman's story and the business about Phil and Sheila Thompson's treasure hunting, where does that leave us?" I asked.

"Us?" Zimmer repeated dryly.

"You're the one who told me to stay behind and then asked my opinion about Matt's story. Seems to me like we're workin' together."

"I prefer to think of it as picking your brain," he said. "Consider yourself an unofficial consultant. We're not partners or anything like that."

"Fine by me, Detective," I told him.

"Then as a consultant, can you think of any reason for Walter Harvick to be going to the stable at three o'clock in the morning?"

"Not a blasted one," I said.

He grimaced. "That's what I was afraid of. Neither can I. But I'm going to take a walk over there anyway and have a look around, to see if anything suggests itself to me. Would you like to come along?"

"I don't have anything better to do."

That wasn't strictly true. Lying by the pool and getting sunscreen rubbed on me by Tom Bradenton would be a lot better, or at least a lot more enjoyable.

But it would be even more fun if Zimmer and I could figure out who had killed Walter and lift the cloud of suspicion that was hanging over the resort, I told myself.

We left the office. I looked around the lobby for Luke but didn't see him. I could have called him and asked him to come along, but there didn't seem to be any real point to that. Nor did Tom seem to be around, so Zimmer and I set out across the grounds on our own.

"I haven't even been to the stable," I told him as we followed a weather-aged wooden sign with an arrow carved into it and took one of the many paths that led through the veritable forest of palm trees.

"You're not interested in horseback riding?" he asked.

"The last time I was on a horse was at an elementary school carnival when I was seven years old," I said with a laugh. "And I didn't particularly enjoy it then."

"I thought all little girls were crazy for horses."

"I guess I was an odd little girl. I did have a unicorn phase, though, which is sort of the same, I suppose."

"Much more phallic."

"Good Lord, Detective, are you flirtin' with me?"

"No, ma'am," he said hastily. "I apologize."

"Well, there's no need to go that far. I don't offend easily."

After a moment, Zimmer said, "Murder offends me."

"Me, too," I agreed solemnly. "Maybe we'll find some answers."

But we didn't. We poked all around the stable, which were fairly small and held stalls for six horses. A female groom in her mid-twenties was working there, running a comb over one of the two horses still in their stalls. She explained that the other four mounts were being ridden by guests of the resort at the moment.

She pointed to a path that led back to the left and said, "That's our riding trail. It winds around for about a quarter of a mile and then goes down to the beach. That's where people do most of their riding."

"Not today, though," I said. "It's off-limits."

"Actually, it's not anymore," Zimmer said. "The crime scene team was finished, so I ordered the tape taken down a little while ago. I imagine it's starting to get pretty busy down there. People never let a little morbid curiosity keep them away."

"More likely to draw them there," I muttered.

The groom showed us all around the stable, which included the stalls, a tack room, and a storage room where feed was kept in tightly closed metal and plastic containers so that rats and mice couldn't get into it. All the boat traffic up and down the Keys in centuries past insured that every island had a certain amount of vermin on it.

"Were you the first one here this morning?" Zimmer asked the groom.

She nodded and said, "Yes, I got here not long after sun-up to tend to the horses."

"Was there anything out of place or unusual that you noticed?"

She shook her head. "Sorry, Detective. Everything looked perfectly normal."

Zimmer looked like he wanted to sigh in frustration, but he just nodded and said, "Thank you."

As we walked back toward the main house, I said, "Back where we started from again."

"Maybe . . . but everything we eliminate narrows the field that much more."

"We didn't eliminate anything," I pointed out. "We didn't find any reason for Walter to be going to the stable in the middle of the night."

"No, we didn't," he admitted. "There doesn't seem to be a reason behind any of this. But there is. We just haven't found it yet."

Once again I felt a little jab of something in my

brain, an almost physical sensation that told me I had overlooked something. But when I concentrated and searched hard in the recesses of my mind, nothing new came to light. Whatever the thing was, it was still hiding from me.

"I need to go check in," Zimmer said when we reached the house. "You'll be around?"

"Where else am I going to be? You haven't said that anybody can leave yet."

"I know." He sighed. "But sooner or later I'll have to. And the more time goes by, the harder it'll be to find the answers we need."

I knew he was right about that. I lifted a hand in farewell and then went into the house while he headed for the parking lot.

I still didn't see Luke or Tom in the lobby. I went over to Tom's office. The door was open a couple of inches the way we'd left it. I pushed it open the rest of the way and saw the vacant chair behind the desk.

I didn't feel like going up to my room, and I didn't think he would mind me waiting for him here, so I went in and sat down behind the desk. I'd been there only a minute when the map of the Keys on the wall caught my eye again. I stood up and went over to look at it. My hand came up and my fingertips brushed lightly over the long curve of islands leading from the Dry Tortugas to Key West and on up the Keys to Miami.

Was the answer somewhere in there? It had to be, but I sure couldn't see it.

I turned my attention to a bookshelf that stood on the other side of the office. I had noticed it earlier, but I hadn't really paid any attention to the books in it. I wandered over there now and studied the titles. Most of them were non-fiction, I saw, and a majority of them had to do with Key West or the Florida Keys in general. I could tell by the bindings that quite a few of them were old, dating back to the Thirties and even earlier. One that had to be at least a hundred years old was titled *The History of Wrecking and Salvage Operations in the Florida Keys* by an author I'd never heard of, John B. Boothe. There was a guide to Key West put together by the Works Progress Administration in the Forties and even what appeared to be a privately printed history of the Bradenton family. I wondered if they were mentioned in that old book about wreckers and salvagers, but it looked so brittle I didn't want to go paging through it.

In addition to all this, there was a shelf of books devoted to Ernest Hemingway, including his novels, the complete short stories, all the standard biographies, critical studies, even a travelogue by a guy who had journeyed all over the world retracing Papa's footsteps. Some of them I'd heard of, some of them I'd even read, but there were others that were new to me, even though they were old.

I pulled one of them off the shelf. It was called *Tarpon Days, Whiskey Nights* and was by Cap'n Jacob Morris. That was the way it was written on the title page, "Cap'n". He'd had a charter boat anchored at Key West during the Thirties and evidently had been good friends with Hemingway. I flipped through the book, which seemed to be a series of stories about various fishing trips.

I had spent too much time thinking about Walter Harvick's murder. Less than eight hours had passed since Luke had pounded on my door that morning with the bad news, but the time since then had been crammed with speculations and revelations, none of which, in the end, really amounted to much as far as I could see. So I took Cap'n Jacob's book back to the desk, sank down in the comfortable leather swivel chair, and told myself I was going to read for a while and take my mind completely off what had happened. I was going to let myself be transported back to those carefree times of the Thirties – carefree in Key West, anyway, after the boom began when the railroad was completed – a time when the days had been full of sunlight and laughter and fishing and the nights full of whiskey and stars and passion . . .

I don't know how long I read before I fell asleep in the chair. If it had been a TV show of a certain vintage and mindset, everything would have gotten blurry and I would have found myself in a dream sequence, back in Key West in the Thirties, dressed in gorgeous period clothes, hanging out with Papa and John Dos Passos and Martha Gellhorn.

But nothing of the sort happened. I was tired, and I just . . . fell asleep.

Chapter 24

"I sort of hate to wake you up," Tom said with a note of amusement in his voice. "You look so blasted adorable, sitting there that way."

I sat up sharply. The book that had slid down to my lap fell to the floor with a thud. Feeling groggy, I reached down to pick it up.

"Let me get that for you," Tom said as he came over to the desk. "Reading about the old days, eh?"

I shook my head in an attempt to clear some of the cobwebs out of my brain as Tom bent over to pick up the book. He was about to put it back on the shelves when I said, "Wait a minute!"

He looked back over his shoulder at me. "What is it, Delilah? Are you all right?"

"Let me see that book again," I said, then realized I'd been sort of abrupt with him. I added, "Please."

"Sure." He handed it to me. I opened it and started flipping through the pages, trying to find where I'd been reading when I dozed off. I had noticed something right about then that sort of lodged in my brain . . .

"There it is," I said as I stabbed a finger at the page. "Bedford Key."

Tom frowned and shook his head. "What are you talking about? I never heard of a Bedford Key, and I grew up here."

I held up the book and pointed. "The old ship captain who wrote this book talks about going on a fishing trip to the Tortugas with Hemingway and some other people from Key West. A squall came up, and they ran their boat into a cove on Bedford Key to wait it out. Evidently the experience soured Hemingway on the place, because he would never go back there."

"Well, I suppose it's possible," Tom said with a dubious look on his face. "It's not unheard of for a smaller key to get swamped in a hurricane and wash away enough so that it doesn't resurface. This Bedford Key might be like that, and that's why I've never heard of it."

I set the book on the desk, still open, and stood up to go over to the map. I leaned close to it and studied the Dry Tortugas. They were made up of seven main keys, but there were smaller islands dotted here and there in the vicinity. One of them might be Bedford Key.

"Why is this important?" Tom asked.

"Because when Walter was arguing with Rollie Cranston at the Hemingway House yesterday about who knew more about Hemingway, Walter said that he even knew what had really happened on Bedford Key. He said it like it was some sort of secret, and knowing it put him ahead of Rollie."

Tom just looked baffled and shook his head. "You think this Bedford Key business, whatever it was, had something to do with him being murdered?"

"Keeping secrets is one reason people commit murder in the first place," I said. "I need to find Detective Zimmer and talk to him. Maybe he can get the Coast Guard to look for Bedford Key. There could be some evidence hidden there."

"That's a good idea," Tom said, "but Charles isn't here anymore. I ran into him a little while ago, and he told me he was going back to the police station. He wanted to go over everyone's statement, and if he couldn't find anything else promising he was going to release people to go on about their business."

If Zimmer did that, the killer might get away. I wasn't sure of his identity yet, but thoughts were whirling through my head . . .

"Listen," Tom went on, "I know Charles Zimmer pretty well, and he isn't going to call in the Coast Guard on some wild goose chase like that, not without some pretty good indication that this Bedford Key is connected to Harvick's murder."

"I'll just have to talk him into it."

Tom frowned. "I tell you what I'll do. It's still early enough in the afternoon that there's time to sail over to the Tortugas and have a look around. I can check out all the smaller keys and see if there's anything out of the ordinary about any of them. If I find anything, then when I get back you and I can go see Charles and tell him about it."

"You'd do that to help me?" I asked.

"Sure." He grinned and shrugged. "I'm the boss here, remember? I can take off the rest of the afternoon if I want to."

"All right," I said. "But on one condition . . . I go with you."

He looked surprised. "I thought you didn't like being out on the water."

"I don't," I said, and the thought of sailing more than sixty miles to the Dry Tortugas, on top of everything else crowding into my head just then, really made me queasy. "But this was my idea, and I ought to see it through."

He looked at me for a long moment, then shrugged. "Suit yourself," he said. "My catamaran can make it in an hour and a half."

"What about your great-grandfather's old fishing boat?" I asked. "Did you get it running well enough to make a trip like that?"

"Well, yeah, I guess, but it's slower. If we take it, we probably won't get back here until after dark."

"That's all right. I think I'd be less likely to get sick on a more substantial boat like that."

I thought he might argue with me, but he just nodded and said, "Sure, if that's what you want, Delilah. Come on."

"Right now?"

"We really don't need to waste any time if we're going to take that old scow of mine."

He was right, I told myself. Now that I might be on the trail of Walter Harvick's murderer, there was no time to waste.

We left the office and he hustled me out a side door and along a path until we reached one of the larger paths that curved through the grounds. We went by the same sign I had seen earlier when I was with Detective Zimmer. When we walked past the stable there was no sign of the female groom. Tom led the way to the riding trail, but less than twenty yards along it, a smaller trail branched off to the right. I remembered him saying that the dock where he kept his boats was over here on this part of the resort, beyond the area frequented by the guests.

There was no beach here. The trees grew almost all the way to the water. In an opening in the growth, an old wooden dock jutted out with a vessel anchored on either side of it. The sleek, modern catamaran was to the left, an old, some-what battered-looking fishing boat to the right. The name *Lucky Boy* was painted on the prow. The paint was peeling in places.

"Your great-grandfather Claude's boat?" I said.

Tom nodded. "That's right. Are you sure you want to take it instead of the cat?"

"I'm certain," I told him. "I'll feel a lot better on it."

"All right. She's gassed up and ready to go. Let me give you a hand."

The dock was high enough that it wasn't hard to step from it onto the deck of the *Lucky Boy*. Tom untied the lines, then hopped aboard and went into the small, partially enclosed cabin to start the engine. A couple of fishing chairs were bolted to the deck toward the back of the boat.

The engine caught with a grumbling growl. Tom looked back over his shoulder at me and called, "You'd better put on a life jacket."

"I can swim," I told him.

"I don't like taking anybody out in deep water unless they're wearing a life jacket," he insisted. "I'll feel better if you do."

"All right, that's fine."

He pointed to a built-in chest with a lid. When I lifted it I found several of the bulky orange things. I strapped myself into one of them. It wasn't very comfortable, but better than drowning, I thought.

Tom backed the boat away from the dock, then spun the wheel, eased the throttle forward, and sent us into open water. The tree-lined shore fell away behind us. I looked around the small cabin and spotted a narrow set of stairs leading down.

"What's down there?" I asked Tom, pointing.

"A little sleeping cabin and head," he said. "Also access to the engine room."

"The head's like the bathroom, right?"

"That's right. You need to use it?"

"Well, we did leave the house pretty abruptly."

He laughed. "Go ahead. It'll take us a couple of hours to get where we're going. There's no point in you being uncomfortable."

I eased my way down the stairs. So far my stomach was behaving, but I didn't know how long that would last. We hadn't come very far from land, and the water was pretty calm so far.

He was right about the head being small. I thought that the combination of a stomach virus and claustrophobia would be downright disastrous. But I did what I needed to do and climbed back up into the pilot house or whatever you call it on a boat like that.

"The last time I was on anything that floated, it was a Mississippi riverboat," I told Tom. "Not everything worked out that great, but at least I didn't get seasick."

He stood at the wheel with casual ease, and I could imagine him as a dashing buccaneer. He glanced over at me and said, "Was that during one of those other murder cases you investigated?"

"Yeah. We were sort of stuck on the riverboat, so the sooner the killer was found, the better."

"And you found him."

"That's right. Luckily we found the bomb in time, too."

His eyebrows went up. "Bomb? You really have lived an exciting life, Delilah Dickinson."

"Just in bits and pieces," I said with a laugh. "Most of it's pretty, well, normal."

"I'm not sure I can imagine you ever being normal," he said, "and I mean that in a good way. You're a real bloodhound, aren't you?"

"You mean that in a good way, too?"

"Actually, I do. Once you sink your teeth into something, you don't let go, do you? You're not going to give up until you figure out who killed Walter Harvick."

"I don't intend to," I told him. "I don't know if being that stubborn is good or bad, but it's just the way I am."

"Well, we'll be at the Tortugas in a couple of hours, and maybe you'll find what you're looking for."

"I hope so," I said.

* * *

The *Lucky Boy* wasn't fast, but it cut through the water at a steady pace and I found that it didn't bother me too much. I probably would have gotten sick in a hurry if the boat had stopped and I could feel it moving up and down on the waves. That was why deep-sea fishing didn't interest me at all. I knew I'd be miserable if I ever tried it.

I sat on a barstool-like chair next to a chart table at one side of the cabin while Tom handled the wheel. We talked about this and that as time passed and we drew closer to our destination.

"Did you ever know your great-grandfather?" I finally asked him after almost two hours at sea had gone by.

"I knew him pretty well when I was a little boy. He lived to be almost a hundred years old. He was a mighty tough old bird, Claude Bradenton was."

"I imagine you had to be tough back in those days if you were runnin' rum in from Cuba."

"That's right. Folks solved their problems with tommy guns."

"But then he became a gentleman resort owner."

"Sure. People can change." He peered out over the water in front of the boat, and a note of mingled nostalgia and regret came into his voice as he said, "I really loved that old man."

"That's why you want to protect his reputation?"

Tom glanced at me and laughed. "What repute-tion? I told you, he was a rum-runner."

I took a deep breath and glanced back toward Key West. "But you didn't tell me he was a murder-er. Is that what he did on Bedford Key, Tom? Killed somebody?"

Tom's head jerked toward me, his smile vanishing.

"Is that why you killed Walter?" I went on. "You didn't want him finding out the truth and revealing it to the world?"

He stared at me for a long moment, then said, "I think the heat must be getting to you, Delilah. You're saying crazy things now."

I shook my head and said, "Not really. Walter knew something happened on Bedford Key. He even had a pretty good idea what it was. I don't know how he knew, but he'd been devoting most of his free time for years to studying Ernest Hemingway. He uncovered enough hints, probably in correspondence and old newspapers and things like that, to put together a theory, but he needed proof and he thought he could find it on Bedford Key. But to do that he needed somebody to take him there. He tried to hire Clint Drake's boat, but Drake was already chartering his boat to Phil Thompson. So when Walter got back to the resort last night, he asked the handyman . . . you, Tom, because he didn't know you owned the place . . . if you could help him find a boat to charter. He even explained why he needed one and what he was looking for. That's when you told him that *you* had a boat and would help him. You arranged to meet with him last night and take him over to the Dry Tortugas so he could search there today. That's why he was near the stable last night when Matt Altman saw him. He was going to keep his appointment with you."

It was a long speech and I didn't have any real proof of any of it. But I was willing to bet that if a forensics team went over this boat with the proverbial fine-tooth comb, they would find evidence that Walter had been here. Right here in this cabin, maybe.

Tom laughed. "Well, I would be offended if I didn't know by now that you're addicted to playing detective, Delilah. You made up that whole bizarre story just so you'd feel like you 'solved' the crime. But you couldn't prove any of it even if it was true, which it's not." He shook his head. "I'm sorry, though. I sort of thought we had something nice going on between us, but I'm not sure that can happen if you can convince yourself so easily that I'm a killer."

"Oh, it's not gonna happen," I said. "I think you only got close to me so you could keep an eye on me and make sure I didn't get any ideas about you. I told you everything I was thinkin', and you encouraged me, even helped me, to go down every blind alley I came up with. But then I saw that book and remembered about Bedford Key, and that made me think about Walter lookin' for a boat and a skipper he could hire, and that brought me a-round to you. I remembered where your dock was, and that fit right in with where Matt Altman saw Walter last night. You weren't workin' on the engine this mornin' at all. You were cleanin' up after yourself."

Tom couldn't muster the tolerant smile anymore. It dropped away from his face and was replaced by a look of mingled anger and sadness. For a second I thought the anger was going to win out and he was going to come after me, but then he sighed and his shoulders slumped.

"I couldn't let the little weasel do that to Claude," he said quietly. "I just couldn't. But I didn't mean to kill him. I was just trying to scare him."

"You didn't put him on his knees and make him beg for his life?"

He looked at me, aghast. "Good Lord, no! I showed him the gun and told him to forget about Bedford Key, and then he . . . he attacked me! He was like some crazed ninja nerd. I shoved him, and the gun was in my hand, and he fell over backward and it went off . . ." Tom took a deep, ragged breath. He shook his head and went on, "Now what the hell am I going to do with you?"

That was the question, all right. He had admitted that he'd killed Walter Harvick. If he didn't want to go to prison for that, he had to kill again, but this time the victim would be me.

"You're gonna have to get rid of me," I said. "That's what you planned to do when you offered to take me over to the Dry Tortugas, wasn't it? Choke me to death, maybe, and drop me over the side.

You could claim it was an accident. You could say that I was seasick and leaning over the side, and I fell, and you couldn't find me in time to save me. Nobody would ever be able to prove otherwise."

He let go of the wheel and turned toward me. "I still could, you know."

"But you won't," I said, "because there's a Key West police boat with Detective Zimmer in it about half a mile behind us. He's probably watching us through binoculars right now. I texted the whole story to Luke when I was down in the head, right after we started, and told him to get Zimmer and come after us. It took them a while to catch up, but they're back there."

Tom turned to look, and I saw despair wash over him when he spotted the police boat in the distance. Then his back stiffened and he glared at me.

"Your word against mine," he said. "My so-called confession won't be worth a damn in court."

"You can take a chance on that if you want to."

"That's exactly what I'm going to do. I'm a gambler, just like old Claude."

He spun the wheel, and the *Lucky Boy* began to come around in a wide, sweeping turn. I could see the islands of the Dry Tortugas ahead of us, but we weren't going to get there.

We were headed back to Key West, where the police would be waiting for Tom Bradenton.

Chapter 25

Tom took his chances, all right, but by the time his trial date came around a few months later, those chances weren't very good. The police found blood on his boat, and the DNA matched that of Walter Harvick. That evidence, along with my testimony, was enough for Tom's lawyer to be able to convince him to accept a second-degree murder plea. Once that deal was done, there was no reason for Tom not to spill the whole story, which he did to his old friend Charles Zimmer, who was pretty upset about the whole thing.

Zimmer sat in a booth in Captain Tony's with Luke, Melissa, and me, the evening after the trial concluded, and told us, "You were right about what Tom was trying to cover up, Delilah. Claude Bradenton murdered his partner in the rum-running business and buried the body on Bedford Key."

"So Bradenton could have all the profits from their smuggling?" Luke asked. Melissa sat beside him, looking around, less interested in hearing the details than in absorbing the ambience of the place. This was her first trip to Key West, after all. She and Luke would be staying here for a second honeymoon while I went back to Atlanta, now that the trial was over.

"You'd think so, wouldn't you?" Zimmer said in answer to Luke's question. "But that wasn't it, exactly. You see . . ." He took a sip of his beer, then said, "They found a treasure."

We all stared at him. I finally said, "A treasure."

"A chest full of Spanish gold," Zimmer said with a broad smile. When he did that he was still sort of ugly, but it was a pleasant ugly.

"Then Phil Thompson was right," Luke said. "The treasure of San Cristobal really did exist. He was even on the trail of it."

"And that's what Claude used to turn a run-down old family estate into an expensive resort," I said.

Zimmer nodded. "Yep."

"This happened when they were on that fishing trip with Hemingway and had to take shelter from a storm at Bedford Key?"

"That's right."

Luke said, "Did Hemingway know about the murder?"

"Tom doesn't think so," Zimmer said. "Bedford Key was about half a mile wide, and Bradenton and his partner, a man named Lawrence Keating, were off exploring and found the treasure on the other side of the island from the cove where Captain Morris put in to ride out that squall. There had been enough erosion over the centuries to uncover a corner of the chest. They dug it out the rest of the way, opened it up, and saw the gold. That's when Bradenton choked Keating to death and buried his body right next to the chest, making sure both of them were covered up good."

"Didn't Hemingway and the rest of the party wonder where Keating disappeared to?" I asked.

"Bradenton yelled for help and said that Keating had been wading in the water when a shark struck him. The storm was over by then, but Morris stayed at anchor so they could fish in the cove. The rest of them came running over when Bradenton started yelling, but Keating was gone and they couldn't prove that a shark hadn't gotten him. Bradenton was sort of like the Clint Drake of his day. He had enough of a shady reputation that nobody wanted to challenge him too much."

"Hemingway never went back there, though," I said. "He must have suspected that something happened, and it made him feel uncomfortable enough that he stayed away."

Zimmer nodded and said, "That would be my guess."

"Bradenton went back later in his own boat and got the gold," I said. "I wonder if the boat was already called the *Lucky Boy* or if he renamed it after that."

"I couldn't tell you."

"Does Bedford Key still exist?" Luke asked. "Or has it washed away?"

"Oh, it's there, although it's considerably smaller now. We've searched for Lawrence Keating's bones." Zimmer shook his head. "Haven't found them so far. Erosion may have gotten them, too."

"Then Walter probably couldn't have found them, either," I said. "He wouldn't have been able to prove anything. If Tom hadn't lost his head and tried to scare him off . . ."

Zimmer's features hardened. "No point in saying what if. That's one thing being a cop teaches you pretty quick. Things are what they are, and you deal with 'em. Anything else is a waste of time and effort."

"The sun riseth in the morning, and it goeth down in the evening," I murmured.

"Exactly."

"What'll happen to the resort now?" Luke asked. I hadn't wanted to go back there, so we were staying at the Hyatt.

"Tom has some cousins who own shares in it. They've taken over and brought in a management firm to run the place. When Tom gets out of prison in eight or ten years, maybe he'll come back here." Zimmer's shoulders lifted in one of his tiny shrugs. "Who knows?"

"All right, that's enough talk about murder," Melissa said. "Luke and I are officially here on vacation now. Right?"

"Right," Luke agreed.

"Luke can show you around Old Town," I told my pretty blond daughter. "There are plenty of things to see and do."

"Key West is a party year-round," Zimmer intoned in his deep, solemn voice.

I had to laugh. "It's probably a good thing you're a cop instead of working for the tourist bureau."

"You're probably right," he said.

I slid out of the booth. "I'll see you in the morning before I head for Miami," I told Luke and Melissa.

Zimmer got up, too, and asked, "Can I walk you back to your hotel?"

"Sure," I told him. I hugged both the kids, and then Zimmer and I walked out of Captain Tony's.

The streets of Old Town were packed as usual, so I was glad to have a burly police detective strolling by my side. I thought I caught a glimpse of Rollie Cranston on the corner of Duval and Greene, but heck, there are so many Papa look-alikes in Key West, who could be sure?

"Are you going to bring more tourist groups down here in the future?" Zimmer asked me as we walked along.

"I might. I set up literary tours, after all, and Hemingway's one of the big names. Plus, everybody wants to come to a tropical paradise."

"Maybe I'll see you again if you do," he said.

"Maybe."

"But no murders next time, right?"

"No murders," I agreed without hesitation.

But somehow, even though I might hope, I had my doubts.

Author's Note

Key West really is a tropical paradise, even though the original Spanish settlers called it *Cayo Hueso*, meaning "Island of Bones". If you're planning a visit, a good place to start is www.keywestwelcomecenter.com. You can also visit the Key West Chamber of Commerce website at www.keywestchamber.org.

The best way to begin seeing the sights before you set out to explore on your own is to take both of the tours mentioned in this book, the Conch Tour Train and the Old Town Trolley Tour. More information about both of them, as well as other attractions in Key West, can be found at www.historictours.com.

For literary buffs, the Hemingway House is the centerpiece of Key West, of course. It's at 907 Whitehead Street, at the corner of Whitehead and Olivia. The website www.hemingwayhome.com offers a great deal of information about the house and its background and furnishings, as well as numerous photos. If you want to know more about Ernest Hemingway himself and the time he spent in Key West, I recommend the book HEMINGWAY:

THE 1930 by Michael Reynolds, and MICHAEL PALIN'S HEMINGWAY ADVENTURE is also an excellent resource.

The nightspots mentioned in this book are real, of course, and I've tried to describe them as accurately as possible. You can visit www.sloppyjoes.com to learn more about the famous Sloppy Joe's.

There are so many things to do in Key West that it seems almost like you could stay there forever and never run out of them. Explore the constantly changing environs of Old Town with its nightclubs, restaurants, souvenir shops, and food vendors. Charter a boat for deep-sea fishing, sail on a catamaran, swim, or just lie on the beach. The pace can seem a little frantic on Duval Street at night, but overall Key West is a laid-back place where people are free to take life easy and enjoy themselves. Be aware that it's going to be hot and humid there. Key West has never known freezing weather, and there are enough cooling breezes off the water to keep temperatures from rising to an extreme, but it's still going to be hot and sticky there year-round. Fortunately those ocean breezes make the climate more than just bearable; it's beautiful.

You can fly into Key West from Miami, or you can make the picturesque drive down Highway One, from Miami to Key Largo to Upper and Lower Matecumbe Keys to Big Pine Key and all the other keys surrounded by the waters of the Gulf of Mexico and the Atlantic Ocean. Key West is really like no other place in the world.

And that's just what you want for a good vacation, isn't it?

About the Author

Livia J. Washburn has been a professional writer for more than thirty years. She received the Private Eye Writers of America award and the American Mystery award for her first mystery novel, WILD NIGHT, written under the name L.J. Washburn. Her mystery novel A PEACH OF A MURDER, published by Signet, appeared on the Entertainment Weekly bestseller list. She lives with her husband, author James Reasoner, in a small Texas town. You can go to her website at http://www.liviawashburn.com and , email her at livia@flash.net, and you can also check out her blog at http://liviajwashburn.blogspot.com.

Made in the USA
Charleston, SC
24 June 2014